# Blair House Cat Mystery
*A Dupree Sisters Mystery*

by

Allen B. Boyer

Copyright © by Allen B. Boyer

For information, email Cozy Cat Press, cozycatpress@aol.com  or visit our website at: www.cozycatpress.com

**COZY CAT**
**P R E S S**

ISBN: 978-1-946063-49-6

Printed in the United States of America

Cover design by Paula Ellenberger
www.paulaellenberger.com

10 9 8 7 6 5 4 3 2 1

For my wife, who never met a book she didn't read

Chapter 1: STALKED ON A SUNDAY STROLL

Washington D.C. is a city filled with important people and a few who like to think of themselves as important. Taken as a whole, those who live in Washington tend to set a brisk pace every day. From dawn to dusk there are people rushing to or from important appointments, clutching phones to their ears while their eyes remain fixed on what lies ahead. In a city where buses, taxis and other forms of transit contribute to this frenetic lifestyle, it's a novelty to know that there are two elderly sisters who prefer taking leisurely strolls around the city. While most people in Washington prefer to save time with a taxi or a limo, Charlotte and Ruth Dupree enjoy a good walk. This is especially true on Sunday mornings when the Dupree sisters leave their church to go home.

If the weather cooperates, and the temperature is just right, Ruth and Charlotte enjoy walking the few blocks it takes them to get from St. John's Episcopal Church to their home. While they like the exercise, it also gives the Dupree sisters time to reminisce about days gone by. Days when they would take the same route home from church with their parents.

The quiet side streets they stroll down receive minimal traffic from the city's main arteries. One of the side streets the Dupree sisters usually take, winds through a secluded block near Lafayette Square. It is along this scant stretch of sidewalk, barely one block, where they pass a few red-bricked row homes nestled tightly together. Eventually they come to one home, a nondescript, yellow-brick house with green shutters and a green front door. The colors help it stand out from other homes. At first glance one would never suspect its significance.

This building is better known to Americans as Blair House. For many years Blair House was used as private quarters for guests of the White House. Newly-elected presidents, former presidents, Prime Ministers, and even leaders of other countries have all stayed at this house while making an extended visit to Washington. Purchased in the 1940s, Blair House still acts as quarters for any visitor who plans on staying for a few days to meet with the president.

While the Dupree sisters are lifelong residents of Washington, and have been in the company of many former presidents, Blair House was just another home on their weekly stroll from church. Its occasional occupants held no fascination for them. However, that changed one Sunday morning when a new resident took a special interest in the sisters.

For four Sundays in a row when they walked home from church, Ruth and Charlotte would let their eyes drift over to Blair House in anticipation of a pair of eyes staring back at them. For the last couple of weeks they'd found the newest resident of Blair House sitting on the front porch enjoying the view. However, this guest's eyes would quickly lock on the Dupree sisters whenever they walked by. Most Sunday mornings when the sisters would pass, they'd turn their heads to watch this individual step off the front porch, slip out the gate, and turn down the sidewalk to pursue them.

This continued to happen most every Sunday. When it happened, Ruth and Charlotte would quicken their pace, while glancing over their shoulders to see if they were still being chased. They would even try to maintain a brisk pace, but eventually the sisters came to realize it was futile for them to try to shake their pursuer.

For the Dupree sisters, Sunday morning walks home were no longer a leisure stroll to be enjoyed. Instead, an unwanted third party was now turning their walks into a race back to their house. There was no longer any time for sharing private thoughts and conversations thanks to this unwanted behavior. It was all due to the new resident of Blair House, a guest with gray fur, four legs and a long tail that snapped when it walked. Ruth and Charlotte decided to name this stalker, the Blair House Cat.

Chapter 2:  THE LAST GUEST

When hosting a social event, it is important to recognize a moment that defines when guests are enjoying themselves and when it's time to gently draw a party to a close. It takes years of experience and a keen eye for human behavior to notice such a moment. After years of hosting hundreds of parties and social engagements, Charlotte and Ruth had become quite attuned to when just such a moment presented itself.

First, there was the sense that light chit-chat and laughter had become more forced than spontaneous. This was closely followed by the usual attempt by guests to share their final observations and humorous antidotes before preparing to leave. Eventually people began to stand, requiring Ruth and Charlotte to gather each guest's belongings and walk them to the door.

Rather than ushering everyone out of the house with a smile and a wave, Ruth and Charlotte liked to take their time with each guest. They liked to linger in the doorway, offer a few words of gratitude, and convey a sense of thanks to each individual. When final sentiments were exchanged, Ruth and Charlotte offered one final farewell as their guests stepped off the front porch and out to the sidewalk before joining the hectic pace of the city again.

Being lifelong residents in the nation's capital, and long-established socialites of Washington, there had been very little variation in how a party at the Dupree sisters' home ended. Having hosted a wide range of friends, politicians and ambassadors over the years, Ruth and Charlotte were quite attuned to sensing when to close a party before their guests grew restless to leave. As the Dupree sisters' mother used to say, "It's only good manners to show a guest to the door before they run through it."

On one particular Monday in late June, after hosting a morning social event that featured coffee, pastries and discussions about an animal shelter in need of funding, the Dupree sisters began to notice those all too familiar indicators. It had been a fun morning filled with stories, laughter and fellowship, but now all signs indicated it was time to finally end the event and begin to bid farewell to their company.

A few minutes later, Ruth and Charlotte made the decision to thank their guests and begin walking them to the front door. Lingering in the doorway, each guest offered kind words, thanks and a promise to support the cause that Ruth and Charlotte had championed. All in all, the sisters got the sense that many dogs and cats living in the shelter were about to receive some much-needed financial support. When the last guests set out on their way, Ruth and Charlotte quietly closed the door and looked at each other.

"I think that went well," Ruth sighed, leaning her back against a wall.

"I agree," Charlotte nodded, and she stretched out her tall slender frame and yawned. "Quite a busy morning, sister. It's been a long time since we've hosted that many ladies for tea. Not that I'm complaining…I think every once in a while, it's a good thing to fill this house with laughter and chase away the silence."

"So true," Ruth said.

Together they walked down the narrow hallway and turned into their spacious sitting room that had been filled with guests just a few minutes earlier. They scanned the room and took in every detail of the aftermath of their event. Their eyes lingered on the dirty dishes, crumpled napkins, dirty utensils and teacups that were strewn around the room. Coffee tables, side tables and even the mantle above the fireplace held some debris from a morning of socializing. Both sisters stood with their hands on their hips and surveyed the work before them.

"The unglamorous side of entertaining," Ruth grumbled.

"Indeed," Charlotte said and she let out a long sigh as she looked around the room. "Well...let's start cleaning up, Ruth."

The sisters stepped into the room to begin their work, but were surprised to find something tucked in one corner of the room. There was one guest still seated. She was casually sipping coffee and looking much too comfortable to leave. It was Lillian Green.

"Lillian?" Charlotte said, forcing a smile. "I didn't know you were still here."

"Yes," Ruth added, stepping closer to where the woman sat. "I thought you'd be off making phone calls to spread the good news. I think you have a lot of donors who will come through for your shelter. Why are you still here instead of sharing the news with your staff and supporters?"

"Because," Lillian replied, her eyes clearly directed at Ruth while she took another sip from her coffee cup. "*She* asked me to stay."

"I did?" Ruth asked and her head cocked to one side as it often did when she was confused by something.

"Did you forget to take your pill this morning?" Charlotte giggled while picking up some discarded napkins from a side table.

"Hush," Ruth whispered.

"Ruth, don't you remember the day you called me about a cat?" Lillian asked, and she put her coffee cup down and pointed at her. "You told me you and Charlotte took in a stray cat. You also told me you wanted me to take the cat off your hands. I thought that was why you decided to invite me to this party."

"Oh my," Ruth laughed, rubbing her forehead with one hand. "I did tell you that when I invited you, didn't I, Lillian? I'm so sorry. I must have gotten too caught up in the details of today's gathering...of course, you're here about the cat."

"Ruth?" Charlotte said, stepping closer to her sister. "I didn't know you were thinking about giving away a cat?"

"We have two cats living on two different floors of our house, Charlotte," Ruth stated with a hint of frustration creeping into her voice. "It's been complete chaos. Our cat, Mezzo, has been very patient but...we need a solution to restore some order to our house."

"Oh I'm well aware of that," Charlotte laughed. "It's just that when we spoke about this the other day you were very adamant about keeping the stray."

"To be honest, sister, I haven't slept well the last few nights," Ruth sighed and she turned to Lillian. "I guess I'm a light sleeper. When it comes to having a cat meowing at my bedroom door in the middle of the night, well, it just doesn't make for a sound sleep."

"So what can you tell me about this...houseguest?" Lillian asked before picking up her cup and sipping the last of her coffee.

"You mean the cat?" Charlotte asked.

"Yes," Lillian smiled.

"You know, there is quite a story that comes with that cat," Charlotte stated before sitting down on the couch. "Did Ruth mention anything to you about how we found him?"

"Or how he found us," Ruth corrected.

"No," Lillian replied, her head turning from side to side to make eye contact with both sisters. "Ruth simply said that your house isn't big enough for two cats and she asked if I could help you out. Of course I agreed."

"The cat is from Blair House," Ruth stated.

"At least we believe that's where he's from," Charlotte corrected.

"We'd see him sitting on the front porch of Blair House most mornings as we'd walk home from church," Ruth explained. "He started following us when we'd walk by, but he'd always lose interest in us after a block or two and wander off. After a couple of weeks, he started showing more persistence by following us all the way back to our home."

"And that's only the tip of the iceberg," Charlotte grinned. "You see, this cat is not just a stalker of elderly ladies. I'm sorry to report that this cat may have also unwittingly committed a murder."

Once this last statement was spoken, Charlotte could see Lillian sit up a little straighter. Despite her good posture, Lillian didn't say anything after hearing the last word spoken by Charlotte. After a few seconds, she leaned forward in her chair and looked at Charlotte.

"Did you say...murder?" Lillian asked.

Charlotte quietly nodded while her eyes lingered on a coffee table that was topped with dirty plates and trays of leftover pastries. Her instinct told her to tidy up. Yet, she could feel her eyes being drawn back to Ruth. Charlotte knew what her sister was thinking without even uttering a word. It was the kind of unspoken communication that only the closest of siblings share.

"I'll start to clean up," Ruth finally nodded, standing up and quickly grabbing two dirty plates. "Go ahead, Charlotte. Share with Lillian how we came to find our little friend. Also, tell her how naughty he was. Now can I get you anything more to eat or drink, Lillian?"

"No, I'm fine," Lillian smiled, sitting up a little straighter in her chair.

"I'll check back with you around lunch time," Ruth grinned, casting a knowing glance at Charlotte. "Given the story my sister is about to tell, you might be hungry by then."

"Lunch?" Lillian asked, checking her watch. "It's still morning. I don't intend to be here that long."

"We'll see about that," Ruth grinned before scooping up more dirty plates and stepping into the kitchen. "When it comes to stories, my sister doesn't leave out any details."

Lillian's eyes followed Ruth out of the room before turning to Charlotte with an uncertain expression on her face.

"So about that cat," Charlotte said with a sweet smile. "Given my sister's warning, I'll say that it's a long, but interesting, story. If you get tired of listening to what I have to say, please tell me, Lillian. I don't want to bore you. Don't worry about hurting my feelings, either. You won't be the first person to tell me I talk too much."

"Well, let's start from the beginning and I'll tell you when to stop," Lillian advised and she shifted in her seat like she was about to go for a long car drive.

Charlotte closed her eyes. In her mind, the memories came flooding back with images that flickered as quickly as a candle flame. Then, once her train of thought was correct, she opened her eyes and began to speak.

## Chapter 3: A PATCH OF STILLNESS

As you know, Ruth and I have shared this house for many years. In fact, it's the same house we lived in as young girls with our parents. I have good memories of those years. Sometimes, when I walk from one room to another, I swear it's like melting into the past.

On a given day, when I pass through a room, I can still see younger versions of Ruth and me lying on the floor playing with our toys, having tea parties, or playing cards. Walk into another room, I can picture us as school girls, reading our books or playing the piano. Even when we entertain guests, I still think back to our favorite pastime when our mother hosted parties. As children, Ruth and I liked to spy on mother and her guests. We paid close attention to them when they spoke over coffee or cards. We'd crawl under a table or hide behind a chair and listen carefully to their hushed tones, discussing the latest political gossip and scandals floating around Washington. Upon reflection, some of it was probably too scandalous for young ears, but Ruth and I didn't care.

However, childhood memories don't just reside in our home. In fact, Lafayette Square is another place that holds a special place in our hearts. Just a block from where we live, it's a place that our mother liked to take us to in the spring. I remember walking around the park on many spring days to admire the brightly colored flowers and the minty green leaves on the trees. Sometimes we'd even pack a lunch, pitch a blanket and enjoy a picnic lunch under flawless blue skies. On occasion, mother would even bring a book, sit on a bench and read while Ruth and I played.

Now that we've entered what some call our "golden years," Ruth and I find great comfort in living in the same house where our parents raised us. We also enjoy taking occasional strolls around Lafayette Square to savor the flowers and the memories of spring picnics gone by. However, living in the past is not how we spend our days.

Despite being in our seventies, we still wake up with a mutual curiosity for how each day will present itself. We like to begin the morning by reading the newspaper over our usual breakfast of muffins, oatmeal and tea. We find the morning paper is the best way for us to keep track of the political landscape of the city. After all, being old is no excuse for being uninformed.

In addition to reading the paper, my sister and I also try to attend at least one social engagement a week. Whether it's an invitation to chat about politics over coffee with old friends, or a fundraiser at the home of a socialite, or even the chance to take in a ballet with a few well-connected couples, social events in this city provide us with other ways to keep up with the latest details that make Washington society turn from day to day. As I try to explain to the younger members of our church, important information comes from lips and not from the Internet.

Whether by phone calls, or by mail, or even through casual conversations, the invitations we receive seem to come every week. Now it would be quite easy for my sister and me to accept every request we get in a never-ending pursuit of the frivolous gossip that floats around this city. However, we agreed a long time ago that the best way to go through life is to partake of things in moderation, which includes social events and gossip.

In being selective about which engagements to attend, I think we're very well informed on a variety of topics and people. However, there are some things that juicy gossip can't prepare us for. One such matter revealed itself to us not so long ago in the form of a cat.

Chapter 4: THE GUEST

It began on a nondescript morning. Nondescript in how, like most other mornings, the routines we followed were fairly typical. Ruth and I shared breakfast, scanned the newspapers and discussed what few stories merited our attention. In my opinion, there is no better way for sisters to start the day. Once breakfast was finished, and our discussion waned, we typically set off in different directions.

Ruth usually likes to clear the table, wash the dirty dishes and tidy up. She tells me it gives her great pleasure in restoring order to our kitchen. While Ruth works she also listens to her favorite political talk radio show, which is my cue to move to another part of the house. No matter what room I go to I can still hear her talking back to the show's host who I think is a bit of a rascal.

My favorite place to go most mornings is our sitting room. I take half a cup of coffee and retreat down the hall to the silence of the room. Located in the front of the house, I enjoy settling into my favorite chair to watch the morning sunlight illuminate the room. I sit back in my chair and look out a large bay window that perfectly frames the sidewalk and street in front of our house. From this vantage point, I like to sip the last of my coffee and watch the flow of government workers in front of our house as they pass on their way to work.

While nursing the last of my coffee, I'll watch the faces of those young working professionals who cross in front of our house. I'll watch their hurried strides, their manner of dress and the rigid expressions on their faces. Taken as a whole, the scene reminds me of days from my youth, mornings from long ago when I was a younger version of myself joining in that stream of federal humanity filling the sidewalks. If I close my eyes, I can still see myself on the way to the House of Representatives where I worked as a secretary right out of high school. Some mornings it's quite easy for me to see the ghosts of my past mix in with the morning commuters that flow by the windows. On those mornings, my heart swells with youthful ambition at the thought of joining them.

On one particular morning, while I was watching those bustling bodies pass before my eyes, I began to sense a small patch of stillness in the middle of all that hustle and bustle. The image caused me to get up and walk closer to the bay window. The stillness I spied was down around the shoes and ankles of those commuters passing along the sidewalk. I stared at it for quite a while, squinting into the morning sunshine before discerning something small and gray seated on the curb. My curiosity was peaked.

Conscious of my pajamas, I tied my navy blue robe shut and stepped out the front door. The air was cool but the sun was quite warm. I stood on the front porch in my slippers and robe and tried to get a better view of the small gray object on the sidewalk. Normally, I would be embarrassed to step outside in my robe and pajamas, but the people passing by were too busy looking at their phones to even notice me. Once I got a better view of the gray object, I took one step back, pushed the front door open with my hip and called inside.

"Ruth!" I shouted.

I could hear the water from the faucet grow silent before her short round figure appeared from the kitchen. I saw her make her way down the hall that leads to the front door. Calling Ruth my "little sister" wasn't just a figure of speech. In addition to being younger, she is also a good foot shorter than me. So when she reached the front porch I couldn't help but notice another difference between us. Unlike me, Ruth was less concerned about securing her robe. In fact, she stood beside me on the porch with her gray robe hanging wide open so her pink pajama pants and shirt were clearly visible. Whether the sheep printed on her pajamas could be seen by commuters was of no concern to her.

So there I stood with my little sister, her no-nonsense demeanor on clear display for all of Washington to see. I couldn't help but roll my eyes at the scene before I turned and waved a finger out to where the federal workers were passing.

"I think your little friend is back," I finally said and I pointed beyond the wrought iron fence that wrapped around our property to the cat sitting on the sidewalk.

Ruth took a few steps out to the edge of the porch and squinted at the street.

"So he is," Ruth nodded, and she glanced down at her watch. "A little early this morning it appears. He must be hungry. I'll be right back."

Without hesitation she ducked back in the house and went into the kitchen.

"Why doesn't someone from Blair House ever feed this cat?" I grumbled.

We'd first met this cat innocently enough on a Sunday. That's the day of the week that the cat first started coming around. Of course, my sister loves cats and quickly felt sorry for it. On one particularly hot Sunday, Ruth came out with a bowl of water which the cat lapped up before leaving. The next couple of Sundays when the cat came around, my sister found a few things to feed it. Whatever she put in a bowl the cat quickly gulped down. Once it finished eating, the cat would leave again for destinations unknown. In the weeks that followed, it seemed to me that the Blair House cat was spending more time at our house than Blair House. No matter what day of the week that cat came around, my sister would always provide food and nourishment.

The very next morning I spotted our little friend again, sitting on the sidewalk, staring through the fence at our home. The moment I stepped out on the front porch, I saw the cat get to its feet and smoothly weave its way around the legs of passing commuters. It easily slipped its narrow frame between the bars of our fence and trotted up the path. I watched the cat run up the steps to our front porch, sit on the welcome mat next to me and stare at me with its big green eyes.

When Ruth appeared in the doorway, she was carrying a small saucer of fresh tuna. She slowly stepped down to our porch and placed the saucer on the ground. The very second she put it down, the cat stood up and glanced at Ruth before moving carefully towards the food. Watching that cat dig into the tuna we could tell it was hungry.

"I believe you've started a bad habit," I pointed out and I shook my head to reinforce my disapproval.

"The world is a better place when we help each other," Ruth sighed and she grinned at me. "Besides, why should I turn away a hungry cat?"

"Because this cat belongs to someone," I mumbled, pulling the door shut to keep the flies out of our house. "I'll bet there's someone at Blair House who may very well be taking care of this cat. Besides we already have a cat, Ruth. Mezzo would not approve of you showering your affections on another feline."

"You know what Teddy Roosevelt said," Ruth quickly answered. My sister always seems to have a presidential quote for any occasion and this was no exception. "He said that "in any moment of decision, the best thing you can do is the right thing." I think that feeding a stray cat that is slim as a shadow is the right thing to do, sister."

While the cat continued to eat, Ruth turned to me with an expression that caught me off guard. I expected a smile to match her genuine affection conveyed in her words. Instead, Ruth had an expression that I hadn't seen since we were young girls. It was the kind of expression I remember seeing in the middle of the night when an unpleasant dream would enter Ruth's sleep. The kind of expression that an older sister remembers after being woken up when a younger sister is scared. With a beautiful morning and cat in our midst, I couldn't imagine what was scaring her now?

"Ruth?" I finally asked. "Are you okay?"

She simply looked at me and gestured for me to come closer. Mindful of the people passing along the sidewalk, I checked to make sure my robe was closed, ran my fingers over my unkempt hair, then stepped across the porch to get closer to Ruth and the cat.

"What do you think that is?" Ruth whispered and she pointed at a nickel-sized dot on the fur of the cat's back.

I leaned over the cat, adjusted my bifocals, and found a maroon oval tucked in between the cat's shoulder blades.

"It's hard to say," I confessed, adjusting my glasses to no avail. "It looks...dry."

"I believe that it's a drop of blood," Ruth stated. "I do the laundry in our house and I recognize dried blood when I see it."

"When do you see blood in the laundry?" I asked.

"In the winter when we get the occasional nose bleeds it comes off on the pillow cases," Ruth replied.

"That's true," I nodded. "The dry air is tough on both of us."

I took a small step closer and got a better view of the dot in question.

"I think it's blood," I heard Ruth mumble.

"Maybe that cat got in a fight," I observed, pointing down at the mark.

"There's only one way to find out," Ruth replied and she quickly reached down and scooped up the cat with one hand.

In the ultimate example of trust, I remember how that cat didn't fuss or try to escape from Ruth. I watched her hold the cat with one hand while closely examining the cat for wounds. She ran her hand slowly around its back, paws, and stomach.

"He's not hurt," Ruth reported. "So then who does the blood belong to?"

"Maybe he rolled in something," I suggested, my eyes glancing back out to the sidewalk and the people passing by our home.

"He's not a dog," Ruth explained. "Cats like to keep themselves clean. They don't go rolling around on smelly things to get all dirty."

I watched my sister fumble with the cat's collar until she managed to grab a small metal tag. She flipped the tag around and studied the inscription while the cat seemed perfectly content in Ruth's embrace.

"Oliver," she began and then read a phone number after the name. She fumbled with the cat and looked at it. "So that's your name? After feeding you for a few weeks, I could tell you were a male by how much you ate. All this time I never bothered to check your collar for a tag."

Together we stood, staring at the cat. Then my eyes were drawn to the streams of people passing in front of our house. A few ladies I didn't recognize cast disapproving looks in our direction. I tightened the sash on my robe and inched back to the doorway.

"Let's go inside," I finally suggested, adjusting my robe and glancing over the fence at the young people walking by the street. "Every morning when we see this cat, I always feel like we're a bit under-dressed to be out here feeding him. Take that cat to your room, Ruth, and close the door so Mezzo doesn't find him. I'll try the phone number to see who the owner is. With any luck, it'll be a simple matter to resolve."

Chapter 5:  OLIVER'S VISIT

For the rest of the morning and most of the afternoon I tried to call the number on Oliver's tag. For every phone call I made there was never anyone to speak to. In between phone calls, it was hard to ignore the interaction between Oliver and Mezzo. Throughout the afternoon I could hear the occasional sounds of hissing followed closely by one cat chasing another out of a room. In short, it seemed to me that Mezzo and Oliver were not enjoying each other's company.

Soon the sky grew into a darker shade of blue, and the trickle of government workers I saw in the morning began to fill our sidewalk again as they headed home. It was at this point in the day that I resigned myself to the fact that Oliver was not going to be just a temporary guest. Like it or not, Ruth and I were going to have a house guest for the rest of the day.

Later in the evening, dinner was quite loud, but not because of the radio or Ruth and me exchanging words about our day. No, the noise could be attributed to Mezzo and Oliver getting to know each other in loud meows and occasional hissing. After dinner, we decided to tackle the challenge of juggling two cats in the same house for the night. Boundaries had to be established. We've had our cat, Mezzo, for many years. Ruth and I both know that she's a spoiled cat who enjoys ruling the house...in her own way. To keep both cats apart for the night we decided to make arrangements for Oliver to sleep in the guest room upstairs, while Mezzo stretched out in her usual spot on the downstairs sofa for the night.

Like two mothers preparing a child for bed, I had the job of readying a guest room for Oliver to sleep while Ruth carried him to the bathroom for a quick sponge bath. She grabbed a damp washcloth and began to wipe the dirt and mud off of Oliver's paws. His head turned from side to side while Ruth gently wiped away the dirt before wiping the crimson spot from his back. Once the spot was gone, Ruth held out the washcloth and looked at me. Our white washcloth now had a bright red streak on it.

"That's definitely blood," she said.

"Maybe it's Oliver's blood," I suggested.

For the second time that evening, Ruth picked up the cat, turned him around and again began to check every inch of his body for a wound. Oliver seemed more than willing to participate.

"I just can't find any scratches," Ruth said running her hand over the cat's back and stomach. She looked down at the wash cloth with the red streak. "I know that blood didn't come from him."

"Perhaps it belongs to another animal?" I suggested.

"Or a person," Ruth mumbled.

"Why would you say that?" I asked.

"Oliver doesn't seem like a fighter," Ruth suggested. "Maybe something happened to the owner. Maybe it's human blood."

"Yes," I sighed, "we certainly need to get in touch with the owner."

"So who do you suppose Oliver belongs to?" Ruth asked, still looking at the washcloth. "Someone in our neighborhood? Someone in Blair House?"

"Where Oliver comes from certainly seems to be the mystery of the moment, sister," I replied, glancing at the phone number on his collar.

Together we stood silent and stared at the washcloth. Neither one of us knew what to say. Oliver hopped down to the floor and trotted away, leaving us with a bloody washcloth and no answers.

The rest of the night the house was strangely quiet. Having two cats in our midst, I was expecting to hear a good bit of noise from down the hall. When I came to bed, I noticed that Mezzo had settled into her usual spot in the sitting room. The door to Oliver's room was closed, but I heard nothing and assumed he was also asleep. As I crawled into my bed and closed my eyes I fully expected to hear some commotion. When I got up the next morning, I was pleasantly surprised to find that neither cat had disturbed my sleep.

Once dressed I cracked open the door to the guest room and watched Oliver charge out in a flash. As I approached the stairs I paused for a second to watch both cats race down the steps ahead of me.

When I arrived in the kitchen, Ruth was already making some coffee. Together we sat down at the kitchen table for breakfast. We talked so much about Oliver, we didn't even open the morning paper nor did we discuss any news, which is our usual way of starting off the day. Instead, the conversation was clearly focused on our guest and what we were going to do with him. I think we both felt a sense of urgency over the situation.

"We really do need to find Oliver's owner," I said before taking my first sip of coffee for the day.

"I called the number on his tag while you were upstairs getting dressed," Ruth reported. "No one picked up. I'll try again later. I think as soon as we talk to his owner, we'll get this matter resolved."

It sounded quite straight forward, the way my sister explained it. All we needed was someone to answer our phone call and tell us where Oliver belonged. It sounded oh so simple. However, like most things in life...what sounds easy when spoken doesn't necessarily make it easily done.

For the rest of the morning, every half hour, we were making phone calls. From early morning to early afternoon no one ever answered the calls we made. Having no luck with the phone number, our focus turned from the stray cat in our midst, to the many reasons why someone would not bother to answer their phone.

Perhaps they had gone on a trip. Perhaps they had gone to the hospital. Perhaps they moved and simply didn't want to take a cat with them. Whatever the reason, Ruth and I agreed it was rather frustrating spending the day calling a phone number that no one chose to answer.

By lunch time I could feel my frustration growing. I had spent the better part of my morning keeping one eye on Oliver and another on Mezzo. We tried our best to keep both cats from being around each other while we worked around the house. By the afternoon, Ruth and I had simply had enough.

"Ruth!" I snapped after locking Oliver in the guest room. "This is ridiculous."

"I can't believe no one answers our calls," Ruth grumbled.

"Maybe we should just let Oliver loose on the streets," I suggested.

"You see how thin he is," Ruth pointed out. "Without us he would starve."

I folded my arms, took a deep breath and tried to lower my blood pressure. I stared out the window and tried to listen to the thoughts swirling in my head. When I finally found a good idea I quickly turned to Ruth.

"I'd suppose we could drop him off at a shelter," Ruth quietly suggested.

"That's not an option," I replied. "This is someone's pet, Ruth. Once he goes into an animal shelter he'll be lost forever. He has a tag so he belongs to someone. I think we need to focus on using the phone number to get more information. Do you have any ideas on how we could get an address from this phone number?"

"We could call the phone company and ask," Ruth suggested.

"Everyone is so touchy about privacy these days," I sighed. "I doubt any operator would simply give us an address for a phone number."

"What about the police?" Ruth suggested. "We could call the police."

"And tell them what?" I asked. "We have a lost cat that needs a home? I'm not a police officer but even I'd laugh at that police report."

"Which takes us back to square one," Ruth sighed and she stood up, walked over to the refrigerator, took out a small container of tuna and began to fill Oliver's bowl for his first meal of the day.

"Wait!" I said and I grabbed the bowl and dumped what food was in it down the drain.

"Charlotte! What are you doing?" Ruth scolded. She looked down at the floor where Oliver was sitting and looking at us both, perhaps wondering what was happening to his meal.

"You know when we have guests over for a small affair?" I began. "As soon as we begin to end the party we always have a guest or two who are having such a good time they simply refuse to leave. You know the kind of guests I'm talking about?"

"Of course," Ruth nodded. "The lingerers. And it always seems to be the least interesting people who are the ones who want to stick around the longest."

"Yes," I smiled. "So what's our little trick to get rid of them?"

Ruth's eyes narrowed and she looked down at Oliver.

"We stop feeding them," she nodded.

"Precisely," I replied, pointing down at Oliver. "We clear the room of all food and drink and wait them out. A hungry guest is usually the one who leaves and heads straight home for nourishment. That's what I would propose for our little friend here. Let's stop feeding him and see if he gets hungry enough to leave."

"And what if he runs outside and kills a mouse?" Ruth asked.

"I think he prefers better food…like the tuna you've been giving him," I smiled.

"I don't think our friend will be content with digging through trash or chasing down mice. My hope is that his empty stomach might just lead him back to his home for a meal."

My words were met by silence from Ruth and together we turned our eyes down to Oliver who was sitting on the floor looking back at us with his pure green eyes.

Oliver meowed for the rest of the evening, but Ruth stayed firm and refused to feed him. Once again our home was turned into divided territory for another night. I took Mezzo and her food into the guest room with me. I quickly closed the door while she ate to keep Oliver from taking any. I remained in the room with Mezzo until she was finished before opening the door. Oliver, on the other hand, seemed content to lie on the floor in a small patch of sunlight that slipped through the bay window in our sitting room. Whenever I walked through the room, I kept one eye on our furry gray guest.

The next morning I got the sense that our plan was coming together. Oliver became more vocal, following Ruth around the house and meowing more frequently. It seemed to me that Oliver was counting on Ruth's generous nature to provide him with one more bowl of milk. Soon Ruth settled into a chair and began reading a book. Sensing that his persuasive skills were not working, Oliver eventually seated himself at our front door. Like many of our hungry guests, it appeared to me that he was finally ready to leave.

"Sister," I whispered over to Ruth.

Out of the corner of my eye I saw her put down her book and tiptoe over to me at the front door. Together we spied on Oliver as he sat by the door and reached out like he was polishing it with his front paw. Ruth and I stood by the door and tried to interpret the gesture.

"Do you think he's ready to leave?" Ruth asked.

"There's only one way to find out," I stated, glancing over to Ruth. "Now remember, we need to keep up with him no matter how fast he runs. This is our best chance of finding out who this cat belongs to."

"*If* he goes home," Ruth pointed out. "I'm not following him down some dirty alleys to dig through garbage cans. For all we know he might just go off to another house to beg for food."

"Be that as it may," I said. "Let's try to keep our eyes open and not lose him."

With those final words, I wrapped my fingers around the doorknob, cracked it open and watched Oliver quickly stand up from his sitting position. His nose pressed against the slender crack between door and door frame. I took a deep breath and slowly opened the door. Oliver quickly stepped out to the front porch and trotted down the narrow path to the sidewalk. Ruth and I looked at each other. Our pursuit had begun.

Chapter 6: CAT WALK AT DUSK

If I remember correctly, Oliver was quite light on his feet. We watched him bound down the steps of our front porch, cut across the front yard and slip through the wrought iron fence that surrounds our small property. It was like his little paws were floating on air when I saw the ease with which he moved. Ruth and I, on the other hand, appeared to be walking in molasses. We stepped down from our porch at our usual slow but steady pace. By the time we reached the sidewalk we were both woefully behind Oliver's fast pace.

"Do you see him, Charlotte?" Ruth asked, adjusting her glasses.

"I think so," I said, pointing in his direction before accidently bumping into a young lady jogging by me.

"Chasing a cat at our age," Ruth grumbled as she stepped in front of me. "Not one of your best ideas, sister. We might as well just chase after a bird while we're at it!"

"Pessimism never won any battles," I snapped. "That's what President Eisenhower liked to say. Now walk faster, sister, and quit complaining!"

Down the sidewalk we went in pursuit of Oliver, looking quite ridiculous to the many people we walked by. At first, we tried following Oliver at a leisure pace, so as not to draw attention. Soon we found that trying to walk at a casual pace was not an option. The speed of our strides increased to where we probably appeared to be powerwalking to any bystanders watching us.

In addition to the speed of our steps, Ruth and I also had to negotiate around morning walkers. The people strolling in front of us made it a challenge just to keep one eye on our little friend. After a block, I was getting tired of the pace. When Ruth and I do a bit of walking, we tend to stroll around town, not power walk. It became clear to me that maintaining this kind of pace was simply asking for sore knees and a steady diet of aspirin and ice when we got home.

"I think he seems to know where he's going," I heard Ruth puff from up ahead. "He's keeping on the sidewalk and not wavering off it."

"For someone with such small legs Oliver does move very quickly," I observed while trying to control my breathing.

"Four legs move faster than two," Ruth commented.

I tried to ignore the looks I was receiving from the people we passed. At one point, growing tired of receiving confused looks from strangers I bumped, I glanced up to see that the morning sky which was blue as a baby's blanket had spread evenly across the city. I could feel my breathing begin to settle and I was surprised at how well Ruth and I were able to keep up in the dying evening light. We were so focused on not losing Oliver that we'd paid little attention to the red-bricked row homes we were passing.

Together we followed Oliver down a street that we were all too familiar with. There we watched him hop through a gate that surrounded Blair House. The yellow brick building with green trim was quite distinct from other homes on this street. It was interesting to watch Oliver climb up the steps to the home, sit down on the top step, and look at us from the front porch. If I didn't know better, I'd swear he had a look of contentment about his surroundings.

"Do you suppose the owner is in there?" Ruth asked.

"Blair House?" I asked. "I...I don't know. If Oliver belonged to someone in there I'd imagine the Secret Service would be swarming that cat by now."

"You may be right," Ruth nodded. "Perhaps he belonged to someone who was visiting the President and simply lost or forgot about the cat."

"So what do we do now?" Ruth asked, folding her arms and turning to me. "Do we just stand out here and wait for someone to come out and claim Oliver?"

"We have nothing to do," I replied, leaning on the fence. "Let's just wait around for a few minutes."

So there we stood for what must have been a good ten minutes. It was almost like a staring contest between us and that cat. We looked at Oliver and he simply remained seated looking back at us. Every so often, Ruth would ask if we could leave, but I stood my ground and refused to go.

Then, without warning, Oliver hopped to his feet. I grabbed Ruth by the arm and pointed through the fence. Together we watched him trot through the front yard. This time he slipped through the fence and resumed his route down the sidewalk.

"This is ridiculous!" I heard Ruth complain from behind me. "Following a cat around town? We need a taxi to keep up with him."

"It's good exercise!" I called back while rushing down the sidewalk.

We managed to follow Oliver around a corner where he leaped in between the rods of a black iron fence that surrounded a slender red-brick home. It was a home that looked very much like our own.

We both stopped and tried to catch our breath.

"Do...you...think...he's...finally stopping?" Ruth asked in between deep breaths.

"I hope so," I puffed in reply.

"Maybe this is where he lives," Ruth suggested, leaning on the fence.

I was too tired to reply.

So there we stood catching our breath and watching Oliver stroll around the narrow strip of yard in front of the small red-brick house. It soon became apparent to Ruth and me that no one was coming out on the porch. In fact, no one even appeared to be home. The front door was closed tight. Not even a curtain stirred in the window. For all the details we could spy, the house appeared completely vacant.

Eventually Oliver hopped up on the porch and stared at us like we were trespassing on his territory. He meowed once then trotted to the side of the house where, much to my surprise, he hopped up into a tree and climbed out on a limb. From the limb, we watched him jump and land perfectly on a narrow window ledge. He turned and slipped inside a corner window, his tail was the last part of him we saw going inside.

"I wonder how he knew that window was open?" I asked.

"Maybe he's been here before," Ruth replied.

"Many windows and he picked that one to go in," I continued. "Yes, sister, I'd say he's familiar with this house. He knew all too well that the window was going to be open. There was no hesitation on his part when he moved towards it."

"Then maybe Oliver really does have a home," Ruth stated, gesturing with one hand at the property. "I wonder if his owner lives in there?"

"Well," I sighed, tapping my hand on the fence surrounding the property, "we can't very well climb over the fence now, can we?"

"If we could get by this fence it certainly wouldn't hurt to knock on the front door or take a peek in the window," Ruth said.

I watched Ruth take a few steps to her right, grab hold of the gate and, much to my surprise, push the gate wide open.

"Look at that," Ruth said and she began to step onto the property.

"Wait!" I called out, grabbing Ruth by the arm. "Are you sure you want to do this?"

"You know that every person in D.C. keeps their gate locked. I don't want us to be accused of trespassing or worse, cited by the police."

"Oliver broke into the house," Ruth smiled before turning and looking at the house. "We're not going to climb through the window. If anyone asks, we're simply asking for our cat back. A perfectly reasonable explanation for why we are knocking on a door or looking through a window."

I reached out and let my hand rest on the fence, which felt cool to the touch. Ruth was grinning and headed for the porch while I lingered outside of the property. I stood silent, thinking about what to do next. Should I follow my sister's advice and look inside? Should I risk an angry reaction from the home's owner? Should I grab Ruth and simply leave Oliver to his home? My eyes watched Ruth climb up the steps leading to the large porch. She paused by the door and looked at me. The expression on her face reminded me of the younger Ruth I knew as a child. My little sister daring me to break a rule. Whether sneaking cookies out of the kitchen without mother's knowledge, or coming home from a date after curfew, being a risk taker always made my sister smile.

"C'mon, Charlotte!" Ruth grinned and she waved me towards her.

"I don't know," I replied.

"I'm knocking on the door with or without you," Ruth giggled. "Now get up here and be a good sister and do this with me. If someone scolds us we'll stand here together and take it like we did many times with mother."

While I listened to her words my eyes stayed fixed on the window where Oliver had entered the house, in hopes that he'd find his way back out to the porch. Of course, I knew this was just wishful thinking. A decision had to be made. I looked at my sister and smiled.

"Well, if this is where the cat's owners live," I began, "they certainly should offer us an explanation for why they didn't answer our many phone calls. I practically wasted a day calling the same number over and over again. I'd suppose they do owe me an apology."

After justifying the decision to myself, I stepped through the gate and made my way up the narrow walkway that led to the porch. I stopped right next to Ruth and watched as she made a fist and gave the door a firm knock. When no one answered, I tried the doorbell more than once. Like our phone calls, there was no answer to our gestures.

"I guess no one's home," Ruth suggested.

"That would be the obvious conclusion," I replied.

"Maybe they went out of town," Ruth suggested. "It is a weekend, Charlotte. Lots of people leave the city on weekends. Especially on beautiful mornings like this one."

"Maybe," I mumbled and I pointed at the window that Oliver climbed through. "If you were going away for a weekend, Ruth, would you leave your window open for anyone to climb through? Anyone who lives in the city knows enough to lock their doors and windows before they leave for a few days."

I stepped to the side of the porch where the cat had jumped through the window. I stood on my toes and peered in through the glass. Since Ruth is shorter than me, I knew she wouldn't be able to look inside. I remember how the sunlight poured in through some windows, illuminating the inside of the home and revealing its details.

"What do you see?" Ruth finally asked.

"I see hardwood floors, a very nice lavender couch, a side table with a lamp on it and a throw rug at the center of the room," I replied.

"Sounds cozy," I heard Ruth mumble.

Then, just beyond the side table, I could make out what appeared to be two legs lying on the floor. I could also see Oliver seated by the feet that were connected to those legs. Just to the side of Oliver I also saw something glistening on the hardwood floor. At first I thought it was water or syrup. Then I managed to lean my head in through the window just a bit and saw that it was neither. What I was looking at…was blood.

Chapter 7:  THE SECRET IN THE HOUSE

We went next door to a neighbor's house to express our concerns about what I saw. The neighbor, a tall slender woman like me, followed us back to the house and promptly looked through the same window I did. Once she got a full view of what I saw, she didn't hesitate to pull out her phone and call the police.

Perhaps it was due to the neighborhood, or the nature of the call, but Ruth and I were both surprised at how quickly a police car arrived. We stood on the front porch and listened to the officers discuss breaking a window or prying open the door. Suddenly, the neighbor who'd called the police revealed that she had a key to the house. When she retrieved the key, and unlocked the door, the police quickly went inside. Much to my surprise I saw Ruth start to follow them into the house.

"Don't go in there, sister," I warned, grabbing Ruth by the arm.

"Why not?" Ruth asked. There's someone lying on the floor who might be hurt. Someone who might need our help."

"I could smell something foul in there when I peeked through that window," I explained and I shook my head. "Besides, there's a lot of blood on the floor in there, sister."

"I want to go inside, Charlotte," Ruth demanded. "We've been to funerals and viewings. We've seen dead bodies before."

"Please trust me," I replied. "Letting you in there would make for a very unpleasant experience, Ruth. The kind of experience that would give you nightmares. After all these years, I know what gives you bad dreams. After all, I'm the one who you share your bad dreams with in the middle of the night or over breakfast the next morning."

Ruth reluctantly agreed to my wishes, in part because she knew I was right. So there we stood, in the cool morning air, waiting for the police to give us some news. Soon an ambulance arrived, followed by another police car, and then I heard someone refer to the "deceased" while talking on the porch. That's when I knew the body I saw was dead.

Ruth and I hung around the front lawn for about an hour. We thanked the very nice neighbor before she returned to her home. While we continued to wait for more news, I saw a mail slot built into the front door. I stepped into the open doorway and glanced down at the floor. While I could hear the police officers talking, the harsh aroma of a dead body lingered in my nose. I tried to ignore it all and stay focused on a small pile of mail that was scattered on the floor.

From where I stood, I spotted a few letters, a post card and what looked like a bill all spread across the floor. I looked up and saw that the police officers had placed a sheet over the dead body. Based on the style of shoes and skirt sticking out from under the sheet, I guessed it was a woman who'd died.

Now, of course, the view of a dead body got my heart racing a bit. Despite my age I do find the sight of a corpse outside of a coffin to be a bit disturbing. My eyes quickly turned away from the bloody scene to the rest of the room. I quickly noticed a few things out of place. There were a couple of items scattered on the floor. A small table was overturned and a chair had been knocked to the ground. In short, the room looked like a storm had blown through it. If Ruth had seen such a messy scene she might have bumped right by those police officers and begun to clean up out of instinct. With officers talking and overturned furniture filling the room, my eyes were drawn back to a smaller detail. The mail on the floor.

When the officers in the room had their backs turned to me, I quickly bent down and scooped up some envelopes from the small pile of mail. I stepped back out to the porch and managed to read the name on the envelope. My heart began to race when I saw what was printed on the envelope. I read the name on the envelope to myself, looked back in at the body on the floor again, then stepped back out to the front porch. I took a deep breath and tried to wipe away what I'd seen and smelled.

"Are you alright, Charlotte?" Ruth asked.

"Stay out here with me." I sighed, looking at the mail again.

"You look pale," Ruth stated and she rubbed her hand on my shoulder.

"There's a dead woman in there," I said, leading Ruth down the steps from the porch and out towards the sidewalk. "I don't think there's anything more we can do here. I want to go home."

"I thought we were going to talk to the police," Ruth asked.

"I don't want to," I replied.

"And what about Oliver?" Ruth asked, glancing back to the house.

"I'm not worried about the cat!" I answered in a tone of voice that was sharper than what I intended.

It was close to noon when Ruth and I chose to walk home. The bright morning sun provided more than enough illumination to make our walk enjoyable. Without a cat to chase after, we were able to take a more leisurely pace and share our thoughts. The only people we walked by were a young couple who appeared to be more interested in their phones than making eye contact or smiling at us. Every so often I'd glance down at the mail I was carrying.

When we'd stop at a street, I'd hold a letter up to my face, look at the name on the envelope and notice the way the letters were sloped and curled. When we waited at a corner for some traffic to pass, I found another envelope and noted the same name and the same style of handwriting. The name on the envelopes led me to remember a woman I once knew from long ago. The memory of her face could still raise my blood pressure. The more I thought about it, the more difficult it became to control my emotions, which is unusual for me. I pride myself on not being the kind of person who puts their feelings on display to draw attention to myself. I'm more private and try to keep my feelings in check.

However, the name written on every piece of mail was rekindling emotions I hadn't felt in years.

"I hope Oliver is safe," I heard Ruth mumble.

I remained silent, focusing more on the revelation in my hands than the stray cat. I kept the envelopes in my hand. The name on the envelopes was bringing back long buried memories from long ago. Memories of a young woman who was my opposite in every way.

"Are you okay?" I heard Ruth ask and I watched her step in front of me and stop. She put her hands her hands on her hips. "You're too quiet, Charlotte. I know how you get when something upsets you? You keep it all to yourself and get real quiet and don't hear a word I'm saying. Is it because of what you saw back there?"

I looked at her while I thought about how to spin what I was feeling into the right words. I paused for a moment and tapped the envelope in my hand while I thought about just what to say.

"Do you remember many years ago when I worked in the House?" I began. "I know it was a long time ago...but there was this one girl who worked in the office next to mine. We were both right out of high school and we were hired on the same day. She worked as a secretary for a Representative, like me. The people in my office used to call her the "golden girl." Do you remember me ever talking about her?"

"No," Ruth shrugged and her eyes narrowed. "I do recall that you talked a lot about the many people you met when you worked in the House of Representatives. I remember how you liked working for your boss. When we'd have dinner, you'd go dropping names like snow from the sky...but I don't remember hearing anything about a...*golden girl*."

"Well," I began, stepping closer to my sister. "There was this girl who worked across from my office. We were both nineteen but she looked a hundred times more attractive than me. I mean, I had glasses and dark hair that I could never tame...but that girl looked just like Grace Kelly. While we worked side by side we were opposites in many ways. She was very attractive and she knew it. I was not as attractive...and I knew it but I didn't care."

"Charlotte," Ruth scolded. "Don't be so hard on yourself. You've always had natural beauty which is why you never needed much makeup."

"Thank you, Ruth, but I'm merely stating a fact," I replied. "She was attractive and she used her charms around the older men in the House. In fact, there were a lot of Representatives back then who moved to Washington without their families. I think that's why the "golden girl" was so popular with legislatures. She used her long blond hair, that slender figure and her blue eyes to her advantage. She was always on the arm of some Representative for social events. She was also known to be "on loan" for late evening hours to the other Representatives. She was quite the scandal back then."

"I'm surprised no one ever wrote a book about her?" Ruth asked.

"Newspaper reporters showed more discretion back in those days," I explained.

"Reporters weren't out to scalp a Senator or Representative like they are now."

"And whatever happened to that.... golden girl?" Ruth asked.

"Like the rest of us, she got older," I replied. "If I recall correctly she married a powerful political insider and settled somewhere in Georgetown. However, a few years ago I heard that she and that much older man she married got divorced. Now, of course, we both know how small the social circles are here in Washington. I'd see Lana at occasional social events and political functions but I never really approached her."

"Why not?" Ruth asked.

"Because I'd steer the conversation to the old days and her...late night work habits," I said and I simply shook my head at my statement. "You know, she left a bad taste with me, Ruth. I saw her cross a lot of people she worked with in her office. As if sleeping around wasn't bad enough, she always felt she was better than the rest of the secretaries when she worked in the House. She always felt above us office workers. That's why I never bothered to get close to her...until tonight."

Ruth's head tipped to the side.

"Tonight?" Ruth asked, and she turned and waved her thumb over her shoulder. "You mean that's who was lying on the floor back there? That's who was under the sheet?"

"I think so," I nodded.

I handed Ruth the mail that I'd been carrying. I pointed out how the name of Lana Granger was typed or written on every piece of mail. Standing on the side of the street that got direct sunlight, the letters were still clearly visible to see.

"As you can see, this was the name and address that appeared on all the mail," I said, waving my finger at the envelopes. "The same name as the Golden Girl I used to know."

"My gosh," Ruth sighed. "I...I wonder what happened back there?"

"I don't know," I answered. "I saw a lot of blood on the floor...which made me very uncomfortable. Tomorrow morning we'll have to read the newspapers closely to learn more about what happened to Lana."

We didn't say another word the rest of the way home. I could tell by the way she was looking around that Ruth was keeping an eye out for Oliver to appear. My eyes were trained to the ground as I thought about the terrible way that the Golden Girl of Capital Hill had died.

## Chapter 8:  OLIVER RETURNS

The next morning, I was sitting in the front room, looking out my picture window, sipping coffee while another parade of young professionals filled the sidewalk on their way to work. As I watched them pass, my mind was still occupied with events of the previous day. I still thought about Lana, but my emotions weren't nearly as strong as they were on the walk from her house. Reflecting on her death, I knew she was as old as me, which meant she'd led a good long life. Then my mind drifted back to the scene inside Lana's house. I thought back to how the furniture was turned over and there was blood all over the floor and I tried not to imagine how scared she must have been at everything that was happening. A violent death isn't what I expected for the Golden Girl.

Suddenly I spotted our small fury friend lingering along the sidewalk by our gate. I put my coffee cup down, tied my robe shut and stepped out to the porch to verify that it was Oliver. The moment he saw me, even though I wasn't holding a bowl of tuna, he cut across the sidewalk and scampered up to where I stood on the porch. During his previous visits, I'd usually walk into the house and call for my sister to give the cat the kind of attention it craved. After what had happened to Lana, I found that my heart had changed in its disregard for Oliver.

I bent down and ran my hand over the cat's soft warm fur. I stroked his back a few more times and then, against my better judgment, I cracked open the door to our house.

Oliver quickly scampered inside.

Our cat, Mezzo, was sleeping on the hardwood floor of our foyer when Oliver trotted down the narrow hallway. I watched Oliver quietly walk into a side room, leaving Mezzo undisturbed. I glanced in at Oliver before making my way to the kitchen, where Ruth was still cleaning up from breakfast. I grabbed the newspaper, sat down at our kitchen table and began to go through each section of the morning paper, hoping to find some clue as to what had happened to Lana Granger.

"Are you looking for a report on your friend?" Ruth asked, while washing some dishes at the sink.

"She wasn't my friend," I explained, flipping through each section of the paper. "In fact, friendship was never part of Lana's vocabulary. You see she didn't really have many friends when I knew her. In fact, if I recall correctly her only *real* friend was power. That's what drew her to the men she…spent office hours with."

I closed the paper and placed it down on the table, sat back and shook my head.

"I'm surprised there's nothing in here," I sighed, tapping the paper with my hand.

"She's dead," Ruth mumbled from the sink. "What else do you need to know?"

"I just want to see if it was the same Lana Granger I'm thinking of," I answered. "I certainly wasn't going to walk over and pull the sheet off of that body. With all that blood on the floor, I wasn't going to even try to step through that mess. But…if it was Lana…and she was murdered…I'd be curious to know what happened."

"Murdered?" Ruth asked. "Why would you say that?"

"Furniture was overturned...a vase was broken on the floor...and then all that blood," I said with great difficulty. "It just looked like she was in a fight before she died."

"And you say she worked with you?" Ruth asked.

"Not in my office...but, yes, across the hall," I recalled, shaking my head a little to get the images of Lana's body out of my head.

"Do you think there's anyone left in Washington who remembers her?" Ruth asked. "Anyone who worked at the House when you and Lana were there. I mean...if she was as notorious as you say she was...I'd imagine other people would remember her exploits too. Maybe an angry wife or two?"

"Most of the Representatives she spent time with are dead," I sighed. "I'd imagine the wives have also long since passed. I think I told you that Lana and I were very young when we were hired. We were both nineteen and most everyone we worked with was older than us."

"Well, she certainly gets a lot of mail for not having many friends," Ruth said, pointing to the stack of envelopes I'd snatched.

"There are some bills and advertisements in there," I said, glaring at the stack on the counter. "She does seem to have quite a few letters, though. With all the ways people use their phones to communicate, there aren't too many letters written anymore. It's curious to see that Lana has received quite a few."

I stood up and carried my coffee mug to the sink, keeping one eye on Lana's mail.

Once I rinsed my coffee cup out, I scooped up Lana's mail and carried it back to the kitchen table for closer inspection.

"What are you going to do?" Ruth asked. "Steal her social security check? Pay her bills? Read that postcard?"

"Just looking at what's here," I mumbled, sitting back down at the table. "As you suggested, I'm just curious about who would be writing her so many letters."

I spread the mail out on the table and studied it all. The magazine. The bills. The advertisements. One postcard. Four handwritten letters.

"Ruth…did I ever tell you it was my job to sort mail when I worked in the House of Representatives?" I asked, while I studied the mail.

"No," Ruth mumbled.

"Back when I worked in the House, one of my jobs as a secretary was to sort the mail for my boss. Back in those days, as you know, people just didn't email things to each other. They took the time to write letters and my boss got lots of them from his constituents. After a few months, I got pretty good at noticing which constituents were writing letters more frequently by identifying the handwriting on the envelopes. A few of his more loyal constituents had very distinct handwriting, which made it easier for me to sort the mail. I even got pretty good at copying the handwriting."

"Don't tell me you know who wrote those letters to Lana Granger by looking at the handwriting?" Ruth laughed.

"Of course not, Ruth," I grinned. "I'm not implying I know who wrote them, but looking at the handwriting I strongly suspect that all of these letters were written by the same person."

"How can you be sure?" she asked.

"Look at the curves in those letters," I replied, and I ran my finger over the lettering of Lana's last name. "See the curves here…and here? I also see how the letters have a distinctive slant to one side. Also, the uppercase letters look identical…in my opinion."

I reached out and pulled the other envelopes next to each other and took a little more time to examine them. Of course, Lana's name was on all the envelopes, but I couldn't ignore the style in which all the letters were shaped. I was confident that they were all from the same person, but I knew there was only one way to know for sure. Without giving it a second thought, I picked up one of the envelopes and tore it open.

"Charlotte!" Ruth snapped, "that's not our mail! You can't just open it."

"Lana's dead…she isn't going to care," I smirked.

I dipped my fingers into the envelope and pulled out one folded slip of paper. The words I read caused my eyebrows to go down and my curious nature to surge.

"What is it?" Ruth asked.

I dropped the letter and picked up another envelope, tore it open and again pulled out the note. Like before, the things I read seemed strangely out of place for the person I knew it to be addressed to.

"What does it say, sister?" Ruth asked.

I reached over, grabbed yet another envelope and tore it open. I read a few lines before opening two more envelopes. It seemed to me that all the letters I skimmed contained messages that made the intent of the author quite clear.

"Charlotte…your face is turning red. Did you take your blood pressure medicine?" Ruth asked.

"Yes," I answered.

"So why are you blushing?" Ruth asked.

"These are….love letters," I finally said, putting down the fourth letter.

"Love letters?" Ruth asked, sliding her chair a little closer to mine.

"Yes," I nodded, my eyes scanning all the letters that were spread out before me. "And they aren't filled with sweet sentiments. In fact, they're rather naughty letters, if you ask me."

"Who are they written to?" Ruth asked, grabbing one letter from my hand.

"They all begin the same way," I replied. "They all start with 'My Love' and no other name is mentioned. Since they're all in envelopes with Lana's name on it, I'm guessing they were written to her, but…"

"But what?" Ruth pressed.

"I know Lana was my age," I laughed, "so I find it hard to believe that someone in her golden years would be up to doing…or physically able to do…half the things that these letters imply."

"Does it say who wrote the letters?" Ruth asked, flipping the letter around and examining both sides.

"No," I replied, and I could feel my face getting hot after reading one particularly naughty passage. "Whoever wrote these letters has a lot of passion and…a lot of imagination to express that passion."

"I can tell," Ruth giggled and she pointed at me. "You're as red as a pepper, Charlotte."

I leaned back in my chair, crossed my arms and thought about the words contained in Lana's letters.

"If I remember correctly," I began, "Lana was married for quite some time. Of course, given her nature she was the one who pushed for the divorce. Other than her ex-husband…I can't imagine anyone who would be sending her these kind of love letters."

"Do you know if she ever remarried?" Ruth asked.

"No, I don't," I replied. "While she lived in the city, Lana didn't attend many of the social events that we do. On the few occasions that I saw her, we exchanged glances and nods, but nothing more. Given our history… I just never had a desire to talk to her. In fact,

I never even heard her name being mentioned in the social circles we travel in."

"Maybe we should talk to him," Ruth suggested.

"Who?" I asked.

"The ex-husband," Ruth answered.

The suggestion made me smirk and I stared at Ruth and just shook my head.

"You want to ask an ex-husband, who is probably grieving over his ex-wife's death, whether he wrote her these obscene letters or knows someone who did?" I laughed for the first time in days. "Ruth, sometimes I can't believe I'm even related to you. You know mother always told you that you needed more tact. This is one of those times when I can hear mother calling down from the heavens to remind you about using good manners and discretion around other people."

"You know me, sister," Ruth grinned.

"Yes, I do," I nodded.

"I just say what I want," Ruth laughed.

"I'm well aware of that," I sighed before taking a sip of coffee. "One of many reasons why being your sister isn't always easy."

As soon as I finished, Oliver streaked through the kitchen with Mezzo in hot pursuit.

Oliver leapt up on the counter, jumped from the counter to the table where I was seated and then quickly jumped to the floor again. Once on the floor, Oliver sprinted up the steps with Mezzo in hot pursuit. I looked at Ruth who, unlike me, was smiling at the activity.

"We need to do something about this arrangement," I said, pointing in the direction of where both cats had run. "We simply can't keep two cats. They charge around this house like a couple of children."

"Now, Charlotte," Ruth sighed. "It isn't that bad. We were children once and mother never complained about *us* running from room to room."

"She *rarely* let us run," I recalled.

Soon we heard Mezzo let out a loud low-pitched growl from down the hall. It almost sounded like a lion cub was living in the sitting room. Suddenly, Oliver sprinted down the hallway and charged up the steps. Mezzo, it appeared, remained in the sitting room while Oliver began to meow quite loudly from the top of the steps. The expression on my face caused Ruth to stop smiling.

"Okay," Ruth nodded, "I'll make some phone calls."

The following day began on a more positive note. Mezzo seemed perfectly content remaining upstairs on my bed, while Oliver seemed to sense the downstairs floor was his domain. On the one occasion Mezzo strolled down the steps, Oliver ducked behind the sofa and stayed there until Mezzo left the room.

With one cat meowing, and one cat hiding, Ruth and I sat down in the kitchen for breakfast. We opened the morning paper and scanned every page for some details about Lana's death. With each section I looked at, it became clear to me that nothing was being reported. It seemed odd to me that there wasn't even a sentence written about the bloody mess we'd found in Lana's house. All in all, I was confused by the lack of coverage.

"Nothing!" I called out in frustration, tossing the last of the newspaper down on the kitchen table. "I just don't understand why nothing is being reported about what happened to Lana. Not even an obituary. It's been three days, sister. Do you think they even know that the police found a body in that house?"

"Perhaps it's a story just not worth mentioning," Ruth suggested.

"It was a murder," I pointed out.

"You *think* it was a murder," Ruth corrected.

"True enough," I replied and I tapped the newspaper with my hand before checking my watch. "What time is the fundraiser for Senator Hawkins?"

"We should leave here in about an hour," Ruth replied.

I nodded my head and glanced down at the newspaper one more time. It was as though I wanted to will the printed words to rise up and confirm the fact that Lana Granger was dead. Going to a social event would provide me with the perfect opportunity to discreetly ask some questions about Lana in hopes of learning more about the circumstances leading up to her death. The fine food and good company would also be a nice distraction after such a terrible few days.

## Chapter 9:  THE LUNCHEON

When we were young girls our mother was quite the social butterfly. She travelled through Washington D.C. social circles with relative ease. One of the most important rules our mother impressed on us was to understand the function of inviting a politician over for tea. She said that playing host to a politician is like entertaining a rose bush—both can be sharp and prickly and will always demand attention.

Since the small luncheon Ruth and I were attending had been arranged to raise money for an election, we knew the politician in attendance would dominate the focus of everyone there. With her advice ringing in my head, I made it a point to sit back for the first half of the party and let the spotlight shine on Senator William Hawkins.

Senator Hawkins was born and raised on the western plains of Colorado, or so his staff tells anyone who gets near him. On the few occasions we've met him, I thought the senator's face bared a striking resemblance to the rough terrain of his home state. He had rugged features, with pitted marks around his cheeks and a nose that stuck out so much it reminded me of the way the Rocky Mountains demand attention from the rest of the landscape. I could even imagine the snowy cap of the Rockies when I looked at his white hair. Over his many years in Washington, I've found Senator Hawkins to be a ruggedly handsome man with a winning smile. However, while one's initial impression of him is generally pleasant, his mood swings could rival any weather pattern in his home state.

My sister and I were never the biggest fans of Senator Hawkins, or his voting record, but we decided to accept an invitation to his fundraiser to hear him out. He was an honest man who always spoke in straight forward terms, which my sister and I respected. Mid-term elections aren't all that engaging to us, but we were curious to hear what the good senator had to say about his upcoming bid for re-election. We also wanted to see the new First Lady, a lifelong Colorado resident, who we learned would be in attendance.

With all this in mind, Ruth and I grabbed our checkbook and took a cab to a nondescript home in Georgetown that was surrounded by black cars and Secret Service agents. We agreed to let them check our purses and wave some metal wands over us before we were permitted to approach the lovely home of Jonathan and Caroline Cooper.

As we approached, I couldn't help but ponder the rough and weathered look of the Coopers' red-brick home. In my opinion, it looked all of its one hundred and twenty years from the outside. Yet, once we stepped inside the Coopers' home, I felt like a butterfly coming out of a cocoon. In a matter of seconds, we stepped from a cool dark evening in the city street to the warm interior of a vibrant colorful home.

Entering through the front door, my eyes were immediately drawn to the mahogany floors that began in the foyer and swept into other rooms. In the few seconds we were in the house, a quick glance around told me that this was a home filled with comfort, style, culture, and design. Suddenly a large Great Dane appeared in the hallway.

The canine stood tall and lean with a tan coat and a black muzzle. He stood completely still and stared at us. I couldn't help but stare at his long legs and how his tail curled high in the air. His ears were set back and his dark eyes studied us. Ruth and I remained still, unsure of what to do.

"Aren't you a large dog?" Ruth grinned.

"I think that's Caroline's dog," I whispered, pointing up the hallway.

"What do we do?" Ruth asked.

"I don't know," I laughed. "Keep staring and see who blinks first."

"Cora! Come!" I heard a woman's voice call out, causing the dog to turn and walk into another room.

A few seconds later, Caroline Cooper appeared in the hallway. She smiled at us and quickly took our coats. Like any good hostess, she greeted us by name and showed us into the dining room where a lovely crystal chandelier sent flickers of light onto the many serving dishes of food prepared by the Coopers' chef. I also noticed that the dog, Cora, was now sitting in one corner of the room. If I recall correctly, the dog remained in that corner for the rest of the evening.

"I thought I remember you having a dog," I stated, pointing at Cora.

Caroline, who was one step ahead of us, glanced over at the corner.

"Friendly, patient and dependable," Caroline grinned. "That's our, Cora."

The Coopers never had children. Of course, there are many rumors as to why, but in the end they got a dog to simply fill the need that children could not. When I looked at Caroline, I smiled at her short blond hair, her plum-colored dress and her pearl necklace that combined to made her look as perfect as a painting.

Without a dog roaming around us, Ruth and I finally took a good look around the dining room. We spotted some flowers in a vase that provided a splash of color at the center of a long table filled with food. I closed my eyes and could detect a hint of lavender in the air.

Curious as to who was in attendance, we left the dining room and stepped into the main hallway. Following my sister down the corridor, I could hear voices in every room we passed. The house was bustling with activity. When we entered a sitting room, my eyes were drawn to a pair of candles burning on either side of the mantel above a small but functional fireplace. A small group of guests stood and spoke in soft controlled tones, rather than sitting on plush chairs and couches. As we entered the room, I could hear guests saying kind things about Senator Hawkins. In my opinion, all the guests looked relaxed, comfortable and content. I would expect nothing less from a party hosted by the Coopers.

Ruth and I had met Jonathan and Caroline Cooper on more than one occasion over the years. A descendent of author James Fennimore Cooper, Jonathan had his great, great, great-grandfather's gift for taking facts and spinning them into wonderful yarns to share with anyone who cared to listen. It's also why I think he named his dog, Cora, after one of the characters from his great-great-grandfather's book, *The Last of the Mohicans*, though I don't know for sure. For events like this one, I have seen Jonathan command a room's attention with the slightest political rumor. The way he shared a story was the kind of parlor trick that, in my opinion, always kept guests wanting more. Whether they cared to admit it or not, guests loved to speculate about the subjects involved in Jonathan's tales, because Jonathan always began a story by stating that it was factual...except for the names.

Jonathan Cooper is Chief of Staff for Senator Hawkins and has always provided Caroline with a direct pipeline of information to share at social events. However, unlike her husband's natural talent for telling a good story, Caroline is a bit more discreet in her manner of speaking. Her eyes tend to go down and her voice drops to a whisper. When I spotted her, I noticed Caroline had firmly planted herself on the couch right next to the new First Lady. I also noticed the First Lady was leaning towards Caroline, no doubt trying to discern her naturally soft voice.

"The newly-elected presidents and their wives keep getting younger and younger," Ruth whispered in my ear.

"Everyone is getting younger," I replied.

Ruth nudged me with her elbow and gestured to the First Lady.

"She's smiling a lot," Ruth observed. "It looks like she's having a good time."

"That's because there are no newspaper reporters or cameras around," I nodded. "I can only imagine what she must be going through. Nothing can get her ready for the fish bowl she's about to live in for the next four years. I hope she savors this evening."

Ruth and I wandered back to the Dining Room, where Senator Hawkins was giving an impassioned speech, his deep booming voice conveying his thoughts on current events, hopes for a new term, and reasons why he supported the country's new president. Since Ruth was hungry, we made our way directly to the table to pick at a few trays of food while the Senator spoke to the supporters scattered around the room.

"The President and I need your help," Senator Hawkins implored, and his cracked and pitted face pushed into a smile while he looked around the room. "The President has just won the White House. He's only been in town just a few months and I only have two years before my midterm election to help him achieve his goals. I want to do more. Two years won't be long enough for the kind of change the President sees for this country. That's why I'm doing fundraisers like this now. I want to start early so I'm strong out of the gate for the campaign season. The President knows where he wants this country to be and I want to help him every step of the way."

While I continued to listen to Senator Hawkins speak, my empty stomach reminded me to turn back to the table and start deciding on some food for dinner.

"Ruth," I said, pointing out a few food choices on the table. "Did you pick out anything to eat yet?"

"I wanted to listen to the Senator talk first," she whispered into my ear.

"His campaign theme sounds like talking about his close relationship with the President," I observed while grabbing a plate and filling it with some fruit. "If he were *that* close a friend I think the First Lady would be in the room standing right beside him instead of planting herself on a couch in another room."

"Point well taken, sister," Ruth nodded before slipping a cracker with crab meat into her mouth, "but I still want to listen."

"Fine," I sighed before filling my plate with a wide range of delectable choices.

Sensing where Senator Hawkins was going with his speech, I chose to leave the room and my sister for a quieter room down the hall. At social events, this is a typical scenario for us. While my sister likes to jump into the middle of a group and state her opinions on matters I tend to take the opposite approach. I like to walk around a party, soak in the people, the conversations, and get a real lay of the land for what's happening.

At this party, I got the sense that a few people felt the First Lady was too soft spoken in her opinions and that she needed to be more forceful in her thoughts about things. I heard some people discussing the need to hold onto the party line in the Senate and that supporting the good Senator from Colorado would help. I even heard one person complain that the salmon tasted too flat, which made me curious enough to walk over to a serving tray on a mantle and sample a piece for myself.

As I settled into a chair, I began to taste the salmon and found it to be perfectly seasoned for my pallet.

"Delightful," I whispered to no one in particular.

While I ate another bite of salmon, my eyes scanned the room. On occasion, I'd spot a white head circulating between clusters of much younger people. Suddenly, in between shoulders and heads, I saw one white-haired woman step into the room. I leaned forward and caught a glimpse of her face before someone stepped in front of me. In that second, what I saw caused me to settle back in my seat, draw in my breath and consciously think about whether I was in the middle of a surreal dream. I stood up and tried to find the answer to that question. Once I spotted the woman again, I put my plate down and began to pursue her.

I bumped by a few couples, slipped between a small cluster of guests, and finally walked around a large group of people listening to Senator Hawkins speak. I reached out, put my hand firmly on the shoulder of the woman I was pursuing and watched her stop and turn around. The second I saw her face my body went numb. My heart started racing. I watched her blue eyes lock on me and after a few seconds her narrow lips curled up at the corner.

"Don't I know you?" she asked me.

I managed to smile at her words and she smiled back.

"You do know me," I nodded and I took one small step closer to her. "My name is Charlotte Dupree…and you're Lana Granger….and you're *not* dead."

Chapter 10:  SWEET DUPREE

In that moment of recognition, I watched Lana Granger turn towards me and look me up and down. The expression on her face made me feel like I was twenty years old again, once more being judged by the Golden Girl. While her eyes studied me from head to toe, I saw her lips push together like she was about to pronounce her judgment on something about me. Her blue eyes narrowed when she looked at my face.

"I'm not dead?" Lana replied, her eyebrows going up. "Well, that's an odd thing to say to an old acquaintance...or did you say I *look* dead. Which is it, Charlotte?"

I simply stared at her unsure of what to say.

"Don't be awkward, Charlotte...say something," she directed in a sharp tone of voice.

"I said...you're *not* dead," I stated in a softer tone of voice and my arms folded over my chest out of instinct.

"I'll still take that as an insult," Lana replied, her eyes narrowing.

"On the contrary...you look very well," I stammered, trying to put a good spin on my comments. "After all, at our age no one can be certain of the fate of old friends."

"Well...we were hardly friends," Lana mumbled.

"Colleagues...in a way," I said and I smiled after my comment.

"Too Sweet Dupree," Lana sighed and she shook her head. "I've seen you at a few luncheons over the years. I never really felt the need to approach you, though.

Looks like you got the same long legs that you had when you were working in the House. What was the name of that Representative you worked for?"

"You should remember him," I said, glancing around at the other people in the room before stepping closer to Lana. "After all, you slept with him…twice. Then again, you slept with so many men back in those days I doubt you'd remember his name."

"That's why I used to call you Sweet Dupree," Lana laughed. "If only you had been more willing to have a little more fun back then maybe *you* would have been the one to sleep with him instead of me. I know it bothered you, dear, but that's how it goes."

"Do you remember his name?" I pressed, sensing that I had cornered her with the response I suspected.

"Afraid not," Lana said and she turned to look around the room. "You know how the memory lapses with age, Charlotte. Names are like leaves…some days they're quite prominent and other days they're withered and gone with the wind."

"I thought I saw something in the newspaper about you," I began, pretending to make up some reference. "Didn't I see in the police log that an incident occurred at your house?"

I could tell my comment caught Lana off guard. She had nothing to say at first. She simply turned and focused those blue eyes on me for a few seconds.

"Not that it's any of your business…but you're talking about my maid," Lana quietly replied, and her eyes turned down.

"Your maid?" I blurted out.

"Yes," Lana nodded. "It was quite a tragic thing. I was out of town but apparently, there was a break-in at my house and the maid was murdered during the robbery."

"Murdered?" I asked. "So...if it was a break-in...was anything taken?"

"You'll have to ask the police," Lana replied and she shrugged her shoulders once. "As I said, I was out of town. My maid was cleaning on a Friday like she always does when the break-in occurred. I had to pay a cleaning service to come in and clean up the mess. Nobody likes returning from a trip to a messy house."

"When I return home from a trip I feel the same way," I nodded. "Always good to spend that first night in your own bed...even if a murder occurred downstairs."

After this exchange I felt someone brush up against me. Ruth stepped in between Lana and me holding a small plate of cheese, grapes and a few crackers.

"Everything I've had tastes splendid! You must try the salmon and the brie, sister," Ruth reported between chews. She then turned to Lana. "Hello. Who are you?"

"An old friend of your sister," Lana answered, her blues eyes flicking towards me.

"This is Lana Granger," I said.

"Oh," Ruth nodded and a slight grin turned up on her face. "So you're *not* dead."

"Afraid to disappoint you," Lana laughed.

"Charlotte tells me you were quite the naughty girl back when you two worked together!" Ruth grinned before popping a grape into her mouth.

"Or so your sister remembers," Lana said, her eyes glancing at me. She leaned over to Ruth and whispered. "Sometimes *naughty* is just another way of describing someone who's having fun."

With that, Lana grinned and walked away. I stood there and watched her step out of the room. I reached over and took a grape off Ruth's plate and tossed it in Lana's direction.

"Same old Lana," I grumbled.

"Well, she doesn't look dead," Ruth observed in a soft tone of voice. "I thought you told me she was the one under the sheet at that house?"

"She said that was her maid," I replied. "She said the maid was killed during a robbery, or so the police think. She also said she was out of town when it happened."

"Well…that makes sense," Ruth nodded before taking a piece of salmon and slipping it into her mouth. "All that furniture you said was tipped over. All that blood. I could understand it being a robbery."

"Yes, that is the easy explanation," I replied, taking another grape off her plate.

"We do live in a city, sister," Ruth observed. "We both know that crime is a problem. What doubts could you possibly have about how her maid died?"

"The letters," I softly replied and I took one step closer to Ruth. "We still don't know who was writing those letters to Lana. I'd be curious to know more about who was sending them."

"Maybe we should follow her around and see who she talks to," Ruth suggested.

"Let's do that," I nodded.

For the next few hours it was easy for Ruth and me to circulate, catch up with old friends, meet new acquaintances, and keep an eye on Lana. At one point I actually had the chance to be introduced to the new First Lady by our dear hostess, Caroline. Once the introductions were out of the way I explained to the President's wife that Ruth and I attend St. John's Church, which is also known as the Church of the Presidents. I explained that every sitting president going back to James Madison has gone there at least once. I also explained that we briefly met the First Lady and her husband when they visited our church right after he was sworn into office. This small tidbit, which I thought would be of interest to the First Lady, was simply met with a polite smile and nod.

After exchanging a few more words the sweet girl offered me a few kind words and excused herself. It was at that exact moment that I knew the country's First Lady was either tired or a bit overwhelmed by this social event.

Towards the end of the evening I found Senator Hawkins in a side room seated by himself on the Coopers' couch. I walked into the living room and sat down beside him. It was late in the evening and together we sat quietly watching the younger guests pass up and down the main hall, speaking with energized voices. When there was a lull in the action, I stood up, stepped to the entranceway and pulled the sliding doors to the room closed. A welcome silence filled the small side room and our ears. I looked at the good Senator. He looked at me. We both laughed.

"A most agreeable silence," I smiled.

"I have to agree," he nodded. "Let's enjoy it for a few minutes…. Charlotte Dupree. That is your name, right?"

"That's correct," I nodded and I pointed to the doors I'd just closed. "It was a good night for you. A good turnout of supporters. It seems to me that you have a young enthusiastic group of supporters out there, Senator Hawkins."

"Yes, they are," he smiled.

"So many of them are a good bit younger than us," I nodded. "Why is that?"

"My staff used social media to advertise this fundraiser," Senator Hawkins replied. "They say they're trying to broaden my demographic base. Get younger people voting for me. You know the game, Miss Dupree. You've lived in this town long enough."

"I have," I nodded.

Together we allowed some silence to build up between us.

"You know," I began. "I think you and I are the only two people in this house who would be old enough for AARP. You, me and my sister that is."

"And Lana Granger," Senator Hawkins laughed.

When I heard that name I could feel my nails dig into the fabric of the couch. There was something about just the mere mention of her name that set me on edge. Still, I managed to take a deep breath, ignore my feelings over being called "Sweet Dupree" and focused on what questions I needed to ask to get some information about Lana.

"So you know Lana Granger?" I asked in a casual tone.

"Who doesn't?" Senator Hawkins laughed. "Half of Washington knows her...and the other half despise her."

"Well said," I smiled. "I do find that husbands and wives have different opinions on a wide range of things....even Lana."

My reply made Senator Hawkins laugh.

"I'd better be careful or she might just find us," I said.

"How long do you suppose until someone notices these doors are closed?" he asked.

"I'm afraid cell phones have replaced natural curiosity," I sighed. "Now if we texted for help, then a rescue party might come to engage us in conversation."

"Perhaps," Senator Hawkins grinned. "You know, a colleague of mine once told me if cellphones had been around for President Nixon, he would have been too distracted with Instagram and Facebook to care about breaking into the Watergate offices."

"You know...when I was a young lady I met that rascal at my church," I replied. "Even if he had a smartphone, I think he still would have found some other honey hives to poke his nose into. Some people have a knack for finding trouble...like our friend Lana."

The mere mention of her name caused Senator Hawkins to smile while it still made me cringe.

"You know, Lana and I first met when we were right out of high school," I began. "We were quite young when we worked in the House for our Representatives."

"Different times in those days," Senator Hawkins sighed.

"They were," I nodded. "However, there are some things that don't change. The political fights to hold the party line. The risk in reaching across the aisle to a member of the other party. And, of course, Lana's mating habits with politicians."

The senator burst into laughter at that last comment and I quickly joined in.

"Are you part of that old joke, Senator Hawkins?" I asked.

"Oh heavens no!" he shot back, waving one hand in the air. "At my age I don't think with that part of my body anymore. Besides, my wife has been an NRA member since we were married. If she ever found me in bed with another woman...let's just say I wouldn't have been alive to be re-elected. So, no, Lucky Lana and I have never...*worked* late."

"And you wouldn't know anyone she is...*working* late with these days?" I asked, simply tossing the question out there in search of a lead to who was writing the letters.

"Not to my knowledge," he replied. "Of course, I spend my days with my colleagues and my staff. I really don't have the luxury to sit around and discuss gossip."

I smiled at this comment. On this point, I felt the good senator was being a bit too squeaky clean. While I knew most senators were busy, I had yet to meet one who wasn't interested in gossip. Because in every piece of gossip there is a nugget of truth that any politician is ready to use as leverage against an opponent. It was a sad but true fact of politics in Washington.

Suddenly the doors to the room burst open and standing behind them was Ruth.

"There you are!" Ruth said, her head tilted to one side. "Are you ready to go? I don't want people whispering about you and Senator Hawkins hiding in the corner together."

"We're not hiding," I defended. "We simply needed…a quiet room to talk."

"Well, your friend, Lana, has left the party," Ruth reported.

"She left?" I asked, standing up and stepping into the hallway. "Why didn't you come and tell me?"

"That's what I'm doing," Ruth replied, rolling her eyes at me the way one sister does to another.

"I wanted to ask her something," I said, standing up and quickly leaving the sofa and Senator Hawkins without so much as a goodbye. "Let's see if we can catch her."

Together we headed for the front door, trying not to make eye contact with Caroline Cooper when we stepped outside. Only that Great Dane, Cora, trotted down the hallway after us. I heard its nails tapping against the wood floor when I managed to pull the front door shut.

Once outside Ruth and I looked up and down the sidewalk that ran in front of the Coopers' lavish home. I looked left and right, but didn't detect any movement. It was like the late evening darkness had swallowed her up.

"She's gone," I mumbled to myself.

"She only left about a minute ago," Ruth stated, looking up and down both sides of the street. "I'll bet there was a taxi waiting for her. What did you want to ask her?'

"I wanted to confront her about the letters that we have," I explained and I turned and stepped closer to Ruth. "How a woman of her advanced years could be receiving those kind of love letters...it just doesn't make sense to me. I don't know why but something feels out of place about those letters."

"Well, we know where she lives," Ruth said. "Why don't we just go there and talk to her about them. I can't wait to see how you explain your way out of the fact that you tore open and read her mail. That will take some fancy footwork on your part."

I raised my hand to hail an approaching taxi, but it drove right by us.

"Senator Hawkins says he is not aware of Lana having a relationship with anyone these days," I said, spotting another taxi only to watch it speed by us before I could even raise my hand. "I know this is election season, and the Senator may want to stay clear of scandals, but I do believe what he told me is true. I can't think of any motive for him to lie."

"Come election season, they all say what they think people want to hear," Ruth mumbled. "You know that as well as I do, sister. Lying comes as natural as scratching an itch for some politicians."

"I think he was being honest," I replied.

Out of the corner of my eye I spotted another taxi approaching. I waved my hand in the air as the taxi drove by us. Much to my surprise, I turned and watched the cab swerve to the side of the road. Ruth and I quickly ducked into the cab and gave our directions for home. As we drove, we began the usual dissection of our visit to a dear friend's house for a social event. We reviewed what went well, what we thought didn't go well, and what we thought of our hostess.

"Caroline is such a sweet girl," Ruth observed, looking out the window at the traffic. "She has a good eye for details and, in my opinion, planned every element of this party quite nicely. The food was wonderful, the house was immaculate, the staff subtle and the people she invited were certainly a perfect blend of personality and profession. All in all, a satisfying evening."

"Yes," Charlotte nodded. "Caroline and Jonathan are both so nice. I quite enjoyed the company of everyone they invited."

"Even Senator Hawkins?" Ruth asked.

"Surprisingly, yes," I replied, glancing out my window. "It's the first time I'd had an extended conversation with him. He was a delight to talk to."

"So he won your vote?" Ruth grinned.

"If only I lived in Colorado," I smiled.

Ruth grew silent and she turned towards me.

"And then there was that *other* guest," Ruth said.

"Yes," I nodded and I could feel the smile leave my face. "Except for that one sassy acquaintance, I had a pleasant evening."

"Lana really rubbed you the wrong way," Ruth laughed.

"Like I told you," I sighed. "I've seen her at social events over the years but never had the desire to seek her out. Today was a prime example of why."

"She had a pleasant enough smile," Ruth observed.

"A smile isn't everything," I corrected. "Sister, do you remember the time mother had Eleanor Roosevelt to our house for tea? We were young girls at the time."

"Of course," Ruth nodded.

"I remember what a pleasant smile she had," I recalled. "She had that big toothy smile she gave us when we were introduced to her. She even complimented us on our hair and our dress. She was very sweet to us. However, I also remember that when she started talking to mother and father over tea, her words were more direct and the smile was gone. She was tough as nails with the way she spoke and the words she chose. That's what Lana is like…only meaner.

"I bet you wish you hadn't opened her mail," Ruth giggled.

"If there's one thing we can take away from this evening," I observed, "it's that we know why there wasn't anything about Lana in the newspaper. All this time I've been looking for her name and here it was the maid's name I should have been looking for. Come to think of it, I still don't know her name. And all of this…because of a cat."

"A nice cat," Ruth nodded.

"That cat is a problem," I mumbled and looked out the window. "I wish he'd never run into our house."

"You're tired, sister," Ruth observed. "Once we get home we can relax and get some perspective on the matter."

"You're talking about our house?" I corrected, feeling a slight headache coming on. "The one with two cats meowing, running and fighting over territorial rights?"

"Yes," Ruth answered with a more positive tone. "Perhaps we should try Oliver's phone number one more time. Maybe the owner will pick up and take him off our hands."

"As long as that last owner isn't Lana Granger," I replied.

I began to rub my forehead as I felt my headache grow slightly more intense.

Ruth turned in her seat and looked at me.

"Charlotte," she began, "I've never seen you like this before."

"Like what?" I asked.

"Letting someone get under your skin the way she does," Ruth replied. "What did this woman ever do to you that has you this upset?"

"Let me tell you a story about Lana," I began.

Chapter 11: THE LEGEND OF LANA

After her first few years of working in the House, Lana Granger's reputation was known around Capitol Hill. Everyone was aware that she gravitated to men of power, regardless of their marital status. However, her reputation grew to legendary proportions one year because of a poor soul who fell under her spell.

Howard Heller was a Representative from the great state of Texas. His wife's name was Lydia Heller. Representative Heller was the kind of man who would fill a room when he walked into it. He was over six feet tall, had a baritone voice that echoed in a crowd, and was the chairman of the Ways and Means Committee, which essentially meant he had power. He was exactly the kind of man who was cast in a bright light wherever he went. Like a moth to a flame, Lana sought him out.

Of all the men she romanced, Lana spent more time with Howard Heller than anyone else. While she would normally spend her time having secret rendezvous out of view of Washington, her relationship with Howard Heller was different. It began subtly enough, but eventually that changed. Being a man with an ego the size of his home state, Representative Heller did not shy away from taking Lana out in public. In fact, I think it's safe to say it's the first time I ever saw Lana uncomfortable while in the company of a man. While they only appeared at social events in Washington, it was enough to start sending gossip around the city. When Heller was confronted by fellow Representatives about the rumors, he brushed off their warnings by assuring them that he and his wife were divorcing, and that Lana would be the next Mrs. Howard Heller. Despite what he told his colleagues, and a few reporters from Texas, it was a plan that I found unworkable. You see, Representative Heller didn't know that his plan was contrary to Lana's nature. She never stayed with one man very long and, I'm sorry to say, Howard Heller was no exception.

If I remember correctly, the affair lasted well into the election season. Predictably, Howard Heller lost in his bid for re-election. In my opinion, the people of Texas simply couldn't stomach a candidate who would leave his wife for a younger woman. After his defeat, Representative Heller was contrite and honorable in conceding to his opponent. It was a side of Heller that not too many people saw: a soft-spoken man who offered thoughtful words for his love of Texas and the people in it. All the newspapers agreed he was a gentleman in defeat.

With his path back to Texas clearly laid out before him, and a disgraced wife waiting for his return, Howard Heller followed through on his promise regarding Lana. One morning he entered my office where Lana and I were working for our Representatives. He got down on one knee, handed her a bouquet of roses, and asked Lana right there in front of me and all the other staff members if she would marry him. The mere question would have caused most women to blush or simply break into a smile. Not Lana. She simply stood up at her desk, took the roses, then waved one finger and led Representative Heller out of the office the way one leads a dog outside. She closed the door and stayed out in the hall for a few minutes. I remember waiting for Heller's low baritone voice to growl, but he didn't say a word. A few minutes later, I watched Lana enter my office again.

She didn't make eye contact. She didn't change expression. She didn't even require a moment to compose herself. Lana Granger simply sat down at her desk and resumed typing without any change in expression. My eyes turned to the doorway where I saw Howard Heller walking away. It would be the last time I'd ever see Howard Heller.

About a week later, news travelled around the Capital of a tragedy. It seemed that Howard Heller had killed himself with a mix of sleeping pills and alcohol in his office. While the newspapers focused their narrative on a career politician reeling from a lost election and a marriage coming to an end, there was no mention of Lana Granger. However, the social circles of Washington were abuzz over a note he'd left on his desk before killing himself. A note that professed his love for Lana and how he would be unable to go on without her beauty in his life. There are not many women who can say they have the power to kill another person. Lana Granger is one of the few who can.

This incident solidified her reputation in Washington. Her looks and her charms and her way with men became the stuff of legend. Over the years more than a few powerful men in Washington wanted to test the waters of Lana Granger, before emerging from her charms with a broken heart and bruised ego. However, I'm happy to report that none of those men suffered nearly as much as Howard Heller did when he lost Lana Granger.

Chapter 12:  GLIMPSE AT THE PAST

After beginning another morning with another failed phone call to Oliver's owner, Ruth and I decided to take matters into our own hands. We stepped out on a warm summer morning and took the same route that Oliver had led us down just a few days earlier. However, without a cat to chase we took a slower pace to Lana's home. With any luck, I told myself, Lana would be there and we could ask her some questions about the robbery and about the salacious writings of her secret pen pal.

After cutting through Lafayette Square, and pausing for a moment to admire some of the flowers in bloom, we continued further down Pennsylvania Avenue. Soon we found ourselves on Lana's front porch. I knocked on the door and waited for a reply. While Ruth and I waited, I glanced at the open window that Oliver had gone through a few days earlier. I turned back to the door and in my mind I started to remember the visions of the chaos and the blood on the other side of the door. I closed my eyes for a moment and tried to refocus.

When the door swung open, there was Lana standing before us. I smiled but it was not reciprocated. The expression on her face was not a welcoming one. Unlike the many times I'd seen her dressed to the hilt for dinners and socials, Lana's appearance looked down right plain to me.

She wore no make-up, which I would expect around the house. However, her white hair was pulled back in a bun, with loose strands tumbling around the sides of her face. She wore khaki pants and a white blouse with sleeves that were turned up at the wrists. She appeared more relaxed than "golden" to me.

"Good afternoon, ladies," Lana said and I could tell it took a lot for her to muster even the slightest smile. "I'm guessing you two just happened to be in the neighborhood and decided to stop by to visit?"

"Actually," Ruth said, reaching into a rather large handbag. "We thought we'd return this to you."

I watched as Ruth managed to pull Oliver out from her rather large handbag. Oliver hung limp in the air as she handed him over to Lana.

"That's not mine!" Lana shouted, and she took a step back from the doorway and raised her hands like she was going to push Ruth off the porch. "Take it away! I'm allergic to cats! Get it away from me!"

"Really?" I asked, trying to keep a calm tone of voice. "That's interesting, Lana, because this cat led us to your house the day we found your maid face down in her own blood. Now why would a cat do that?"

"They're dumb animals," Lana grunted while she pinched her nose shut and stepped back into her house. "How am I supposed to know? Now please take your cat and go before I start sneezing."

"This cat has a phone number on its tag," Ruth continued, fumbling with the collar. "Does this look like your number?"

Lana held her breath, glanced at the number on the collar, then stepped back from the doorway shaking her head.

"No!" she blurted out and she stopped pinching her nose. "That's not my cat and it's not my phone number."

"How do we know you're telling the truth?" Ruth asked, holding Oliver close to Lana.

"You'll know when I start coughing and sneezing," Lana complained. She walked back to her purse, picked out her cell phone and turned it on and handed it to me. "Here...call the number and see if my phone rings or vibrates."

I did exactly as she suggested, with some help from Lana in getting the dial tone. Once I called the number, I heard it ring on our phone, but Lana's phone remained silent. I stepped closer to Lana and handed her phone back. Judging by how the screen was lit it appeared to me that Lana was being truthful. It appeared that the phone number didn't belong to her.

"Very well," I smiled, powering down my phone. "Sorry to bother you, Lana. We're just trying to be good neighbors and return a cat to its home. We thought you were the owner but it appears we're wrong. I guess we'll try another house."

I gestured to Ruth who tucked Oliver back into her large shoulder bag and zipped it shut just enough so he wouldn't escape.

"Charlotte told me about your maid," Ruth stated. "It must make you nervous living here by yourself after such a violent crime took place."

"I have a gun," Lana quickly replied, stepping back into the doorway. "After all, a lady has to take care of herself in this town. Anyone breaks into my house while I'm here...they'll regret it."

"You don't sound all that upset about what happened," I observed.

"The maid was only with me for a few weeks," Lana said. "We didn't really get to know each other all that well. In fact, we barely spoke. Now if you ask me, I suspect Maria might have had a background of trouble. I mean the agency she comes from does background checks on their employees, but that only goes so far. It won't tell the whole story of someone's past. I'm just grateful that dried blood didn't stain my hardwood floors."

"Yes," Ruth smirked, "glad the floors are okay."

"So you don't think someone was trying to rob your house?" I asked.

"I'm retired like you two," Lana explained. "All of my money is in the bank or in investments. I keep very little cash around to live on. No, there would be nothing in my house worth stealing. If the killer didn't know that before the first burglary, they certainly knew it after looking around my house and tearing it up. They won't be back."

I looked at Lana speaking with such strength about that terrible event. If I closed my eyes, I swear she would have sounded like the same Lana I used to know as a young woman. The one who, as least once a day, would strut into my office with as much confidence and self-assurance as any nineteen-year old could have in herself. The image caused me to laugh a little, which caught Lana off guard.

"Do you find this funny, Charlotte?" she asked.

"Knowing you as long as I have, I thought maybe a jealous wife might have come in here and trashed your house in a rage. You don't think that's still a possibility, do you? Is your past catching up with you, Lana? Is there a disgruntled wife in the picture today?"

Now it was Lana's turn to laugh.

"Oh, Sweet Dupree, are you asking what I think you're asking?" she laughed. "My looks have been gone for quite some time. The days of sleeping around ended for me a long time ago. One reaches a certain age when that type of behavior goes from being an asset to being pathetic. I can assure you that my dignity knew when it was time to stop."

In that moment, I sensed another presence in the room. I scanned the room from the doorway. My eyes were drawn to an adjoining room where I spied what I can only describe as a ghostly figure lingering in the shadows.

What I saw was a tall lean figure with piercing blue eyes staring at me from the shadows. Her arms were folded across her chest. Her long blond hair spilled over her shoulders. Her skin was milky white. She looked all of twenty-one to me. She also looked like a younger version of Lana.

Who is that lovely young lady?" I asked and I stepped into the room and gestured with my hand towards the shadows.

Lana's eyes grew narrow and she shot a look of disapproval in my direction. She turned and looked back at the younger version of herself concealed by the dim light.

"That's my granddaughter," Lana said and she waved the young woman into the room. "Ruth and Charlotte, this is Megan. She lives here with me while she finishes an internship. Fortunately she was working when the break-in occurred."

Watching the granddaughter enter the room was quite surreal to me. It was like watching a memory come to life. I was unaware of where Ruth was in that moment. When I saw the granddaughter step into the light I was entranced. Part of me felt like I'd been transported back sixty years. It was like I were twenty years old again looking at the Lana Granger I knew in my youth. The likeness between grandmother and granddaughter was stunning.

"Hello," I managed to blurt out and I walked over and quickly shook the young lady's hand. "My name is Charlotte Dupree. This is my sister, Ruth. I've known your grandmother for many years."

"So you're friends?" she asked.

"I wouldn't say that," Lana replied.

"We worked together…many years ago," I stated.

"If you worked with grandma for that long then you must be patient," Megan replied with the slightest hint of a smile. "I know how headstrong and bossy my grandmother can be. If you've known her for that long, I'd imagine you've already seen that side of her."

I could only smile and nod at Megan's comment. I was afraid if I opened my mouth I'd say too much in reply.

"So your grandmother said you're serving an internship?" Ruth said.

"I work at the House of Representatives," Megan answered.

I couldn't control my eyebrows when I heard her answer. I could feel them shoot straight up on my face. The irony wasn't lost on me at all. My eyes went directly to Lana and the expression on my face must have told her what I thought about her choice of internship.

"So you're a Capital Hill pigeon," I said, still looking at Lana.

"A what?" Megan asked.

"Your grandmother and I used to call interns in the House pigeons," I recalled.

"Why?" Megan asked.

"Because of lunch," I smiled, "isn't that right, Lana?"

Lana slowly nodded.

"I…I don't understand," Megan confessed.

"Every year we worked in the House of Representatives your grandmother and I noticed how the interns would sit in groups in the cafeteria," I recalled. "Now back then college interns weren't paid, so they'd come into the House cafeteria starving. It was like watching pigeons huddle together to eat bread crumbs. They'd sit shoulder to shoulder around one table, with heads down eating everything they could. They wouldn't even speak to each other because they'd be too busy shoving food into their mouths. Are you being paid for your internship?"

"A little," Megan replied, her eyes glancing down at the floor.

"Good," I nodded, and I turned my eyes back to Lana. "Nice to see the family business is being passed on"

"It actually skipped a generation," Lana corrected. "My son didn't have the chops to work in politics. He grew up to be a teacher. Now Megan, on the other hand, she's a natural. She's driven and enjoys being around power…just like her grandma."

"And we both know what that means," I mumbled to Ruth.

"Well," Lana said, casting a smile over to her granddaughter, "we have things to do, Dupree Sisters. Thank you for bringing that cat around and making my eyes water…but I'm afraid we simply can't help you. Please close the door on the way out when you leave."

"Don't you even have the manners to say a proper goodbye and close your own door?" Ruth asked. "When we have guests we at least wish them a good day."

"Manners are for people who matter," Lana shot back before taking her granddaughter by the hand and leading her into another room.

Ruth stepped out first, but I lingered in the doorway for a few minutes more. I watched how Lana and her granddaughter stood in the shadows whispering about something. Both women looked around and made eye contact with me just as I was closing the front door. It struck me that while the expression on the granddaughter's face was vacant, the grandmother's expression was one of annoyance that I was watching them. I closed the door but remained on the front step to consider everything that had happened.

"Rude thing!" Ruth snapped and she pointed back at the door. "I can see why you never sought her out at parties. Not even walking us to the door or wishing us a good day. Your friend Lana has no manners whatsoever!"

"Oh, she has manners and lots of charm," I nodded. "She just keeps it in reserve."

"Let's go home," Ruth sighed, waving her purse in the air. "My arm is killing me from carrying this cat."

I nodded while I thought about Oliver, the blood on his paws, and the fact that Lana was sharing the house with the granddaughter.

"I'm curious," I finally spoke up while we cut through Lafayette Square Park. "Lana said she was traveling when her maid was killed. Do you think the granddaughter, Megan, was home when it happened? I mean I'm certain she had to stick around here if she's interning in the House."

"I don't know," Ruth shrugged, and she switched hands for carrying Oliver in her bag.

"What if she was in the house when it happened?" I asked. "After all, we do have some racy letters addressed to Lana. I think I'd like to learn more about the granddaughter. Tomorrow I want to make some phone calls. I want to find out which Representative that girl is working for. I also want to know if she's been carrying on the family business in the bedroom, too."

Chapter 13: LUNCH BREAK

The clock on the mantle began to chime, interrupting Charlotte's train of thought. Judging by the number of rings she heard, along with her dry mouth, Charlotte could tell it was noon. She paused in her recollections and sat back in her seat and turned to Ruth, who stood up and looked at both Charlotte and Lillian.

"I realize we just ate a few hours ago, but it's noon," Ruth announced. "Can I get anyone a drink or perhaps some fruit or a vegetable tray with dip?"

"I'll take some tea," Charlotte said, gently rubbing her throat. "I just got over a cold last week and talking so much is taking a toll on my throat I'm afraid."

"And for you, Lillian?" Ruth asked.

"I'm fine, thank you," Lillian replied.

Ruth stepped out of the room for the kitchen.

"Well," Lillian began. "If you have a sore throat I can always take the cat with me and come back another day. It really is a fascinating story. I must say that Lana character sounds like a bad egg to me. I still can't believe your cat led you to a dead body. That must have been so uncomfortable for you to see."

"I only caught a glimpse," Charlotte nodded. "It was just out of the corner of my eye. Had I been standing right over the mess and staring at it...I think it might have been more upsetting to me. At my age, I've seen a good many bodies in coffins. I tell myself that the maid on the ground was no different...minus the blood of course."

Ruth returned carrying a tray with three cups of tea. She handed one to Charlotte, kept the other one for herself and left one on the tray for Lillian.

"That's in case you change your mind," Ruth smiled to Lillian before pointing down at the teacup on the tray.

As Charlotte took her first sip she noticed that Oliver had hopped on the couch and was curled up next to Lillian. It only took Lillian a few seconds before she was stroking the cat with one hand and smiling at his contented purring.

"What a good cat," Lillian whispered.

"Now if you change your mind, Lillian, please tell me. I'll be more than happy to get you something to eat, too," Ruth stated before taking a tentative sip from her steaming teacup.

"You'll be the first to know," Lillian smiled at Ruth. She leaned forward in her seat a bit and looked directly at Charlotte. "So tell me what happened next. You had these letters, a rude woman named Lana and her dead maid. What happened next? Did you give up?"

"We never give up," Ruth replied, glancing over to Charlotte. "Like James Garfield said, 'a pound of pluck is worth a ton of luck.' We've always had a lot of pluck in our character. Our mother would often tell us that determination can be as powerful as the Republican symbol and as stubborn as the Democratic symbol. I don't know what that makes us, but once we start something…we see it through."

"In this particular matter we had a lot of pieces that didn't seem to fit," Charlotte stated. "We needed some help in learning more about Lana's granddaughter. And I knew just the person to call."

Charlotte carefully dropped two sugar cubes in her teacup and sipped it again, finding the taste more to her liking. She sat back in her seat, holding her teacup in both hands while her mind drifted back to the next memory in her story. Once she had her recollections in the right order, she looked at Lillian and smiled.

"If you're ready, I'll continue."

Chapter 14:  THE HOUSE

According to a newspaper article Ruth and I read one morning, the oldest ranking member of Congress had announced her retirement. Representative Martha Swann from Maine had been elected to Congress back in the days when women were struggling for equal rights. She had been a symbol for generations of women and sponsored many pieces of legislation to help level the playing field in establishing equal rights. Now that she was retiring, there was a great swell of thanks coming from women around the country.

While I wanted the opportunity to thank Representative Swann for her years of service, I also saw her as a good resource. As far as I was concerned, Representative Swann had been in the House long enough to know the lay of the land. She knew which members of the House were honest and hard working. She also knew which ones were there to simply indulge in the trappings of power. In short, I thought she'd know which members had a reputation for fooling around with their staffers.

After a few phone calls we learned that Representative Swann was planning to attend a small function at Blair House the following week. As anyone who lives in Washington knows, Blair House is famous for being associated with the White House.

Former Presidents, Prime Ministers, even Presidents of other countries have all stayed at the simple yellow bricked home on Pennsylvania Avenue. Built in 1824, its structure always struck me as being unassuming when compared with the other homes along Pennsylvania Avenue.

After a few carefully placed phone calls, Ruth and I were fortunate enough to secure two invitations. The morning of the event we walked from our home to Blair House under bright sunny skies. It was a beautiful morning to mingle and people watch. For the many times we had walked by Blair House, the gate around the property was always closed. Thus, on this particular morning, it was interesting to see that the black iron gate surrounding the property was open for a change. Another sight we weren't accustomed to seeing was Secret Service agents lingering along the street, speaking into radios and looking around from the front porch of Blair House.

When Ruth and I stopped in front of the gate we were greeted by a lovely young woman who spoke with a southern drawl. She wore a bright red dress with matching heels; her long dark hair tumbled over one shoulder. She held her hands in front of her waist and offered a measured smile to Ruth and me when we approached the gate.

"Mornin,' ladies?" she smiled. "Y'all here by invitation?"

"We are," I answered.

Ruth handed over the invitations and we watched the young lady's smile reveal a  set of perfectly straight bright white teeth while she looked over our summons. Her blue eyes turned up to us, her smile faded and she nodded one time.

"Welcome, ladies," she said with a sweet voice and flipped her dark hair back over her shoulder for good measure.

If you know its history, walking up to Blair House is quite an experience. Named after the second owner of the house, Francis Blair, this was where his family lived in the early 1800s. The home stayed in the family for many generations. Since he was well thought of as a journalist, Blair stood on this front porch many times to talk with visitors like Presidents Andrew Jackson and Martin Van Buren. Presidents and politicians all sought out Blair's opinion on matters. Blair's son, Montgomery, even used the home for informal conversations with President Lincoln while serving in his cabinet.

The home was never officially associated with the White House until Eleanor Roosevelt suggested it be purchased in 1942 as a place for guests of the President to stay. From then on, many world leaders, and former Presidents, have occupied Blair House. Now Ruth and I were about to accomplish the same feat.

When attending a social event my eyes are instinctively drawn to the faces of the other guests in attendance. It's almost like scanning a menu for the best choices to feast on. However, instead of considering what guests to talk to for the juiciest gossip, my attention was drawn to the rooms and the objects contained in Blair House.

Silver candlestick holders in one room that had once belonged to John Hancock. A drunkard, or cup, that was owned by Paul Revere. Even a portrait of Abraham Lincoln, the last image of him captured on canvas before his assassination. It was one of those rare occasions when Ruth and I found our surroundings more fascinating than the people who brushed by us.

Eventually, we found Representative Swann standing in the Lincoln Room. With short cropped white hair, glasses, and barely five feet tall, she was not all that visible when we first entered the room. However, when I listened to her talk to two young men about her passion for preserving the past, and the need for funding preservation work at Blair House, I knew I recognized that voice. When Ruth and I approached, we stood next to the young men and began to make eye contact with Representative Swann while she spoke. The second she made eye contact with us, she paused in her discourse.

"Good afternoon, ladies," Representative Swann said with a smile, "I was just telling these guests that this is the room where Robert E. Lee was offered the command of the Union Army. Oh, how many lives would have been spared had he agreed to that offer."

"So true," I mentioned. "I was just telling my sister how remarkable it is to walk around here and find a cup or a candlestick holder and know its historical value."

My words, and the passion they conveyed for history, made her smile.

"I'm Martha Swann. What is your name?" Representative Swann asked.

"My name is Charlotte Dupree," I smiled. "This is my sister, Ruth. I don't think we've been formally introduced but I know we've crossed paths over the years."

"I'd imagine I've crossed paths with everyone in this town," Swann laughed. "The trappings of having worked in Washington for nearly fifty years I'm afraid."

"I can still recall the year you were first elected," I continued. "You were a symbol to women in this country when they really needed one. There was a time in this country when women desperately needed to know that it was possible to break through the barriers set up by men in Washington. You were one of those people who broke through that barrier the day they elected you. You inspired so many others when you came here and served with such dignity. That's why I've always had a great admiration for you."

"Well, thank you," Swann replied. "I know it sounds clichéd, but I never get tired of hearing such kind words about my service."

"As well you shouldn't," I nodded and gestured around the room. "So you're here to support Blair House?"

"As with anything that's been in Washington too long," Swann sighed, her eyes turning around the room, "I'm afraid Blair House is showing its age. This building needs some love and attention. The upkeep for this kind of a national treasure doesn't come at a cheap price. So yes, I'm here simply as a donor today. No speeches...just here to support preserving what I believe to be a national treasure."

"Very good," I said and I couldn't' help but turn my eyes to the two young men by her side. "May I ask you something...woman to woman?"

I watched as Representative Swann turned towards the young men and waved them away with the back of her hand. The young men looked at each other before wandering off with their phones in their hands.

"Are they security?" Ruth asked.

"Two interns on my staff," Swann said with a matter of fact tone. "I thought I'd bring them along so they could appreciate the history of this place. Unfortunately, they've been too distracted by their phones beeping to appreciate the artifacts around them. Most disappointing but that's what young people are like these days. At my age, I feel like their grandmother when I have to tell them to look at me and not their phones."

"I see your point," I smiled. "You know, since you brought up the topic of interns I was curious about a young lady interning in the House."

"There are so many," Swann sighed and she shook her head.

"I realize that," I nodded. "Let me approach this question from a different perspective. As someone who worked in the House during the 50s and 60s I can easily recall those Representatives who were prone to rascaling around with their interns. Is that still a problem that you see in the House?"

"*That*...is a delicate question to answer," Swann stated and she took one step closer to me.

"And that's why I waited for you to dismiss your young men...and their phones," I smiled. "It's also why I'm using the softest voice I can muster in a room swirling with activity."

"Why would you ask me such a question?" Swann finally stated.

"I have a friend whose granddaughter is serving an internship in the House," I began, knowing full well that referring to Lana as a "friend" was a stretch at best.

"And what is your friend's name?" Swann asked.

"Lana Granger," I quickly replied. "I'm afraid that her granddaughter might have become...*involved* with someone in the House. I'm just trying to help Lana look out for the welfare of her granddaughter."

Representative Swann remained silent for a few seconds and stared at me. Then I noticed a small smile work its way across her wrinkled cheeks.

"I knew a Lana Granger," Swann remarked. "If it's *that* Lana Granger who you're talking about...I don't think she would be too upset if her granddaughter is having a romantic fling."

"Don't be so quick to associate the sins of the grandmother with the granddaughter," Ruth replied. "Older men take advantage of younger ladies. It's a story as old as time. You know that as well as I do."

"Well," Swann began, checking her watch. "I am aware of some Representatives in the House who will take advantage of young interns for...questionable motives. If you worked in the House, Miss Dupree, you know as well as I that not every member of Congress is a good and honorable person. There are some rotten apples in the bunch. I have a few rotten apples in mind. Let me make some phone calls and I'll get back to you."

"I'm certain Lana will appreciate any help you can give," Ruth said.

Representative Swann stepped close to both of us and in a hushed voice said, "I'm not doing it for your friend...I'm doing it for the granddaughter."

With those final words, she turned and walked away.

"We don't even know if Megan is carrying on with a Representative?" Ruth stated. "Why would you ask her to check on such a thing?"

"There are many men in the House," I quietly pointed out. "If Megan is anything like her grandmother, she may have come across a powerful man looking for a young thing like her. Call it an old itch to scratch, sister. Let's just wait for Representative Swann's call and go from there."

Chapter 15: THE GOLDEN GIRL EFFECT

The following day I was quite surprised to get a phone call from Representative Swann herself. She explained to me that Lana's granddaughter, Megan, was working for Representative Tempest Hash of New Jersey. The name caught me off guard because I was expecting Megan to be in a romance with a male Representative, especially after reading those letters. When I heard Representative Hash's name it simply didn't match with what I had imagined. Especially after reading one letter that referenced a wife who is "as cold as the reflecting pond in January." I shared the news with Ruth over breakfast and we considered what that meant.

"A man is writing these letters," I said, waving one envelope in the air.

"There are too many men in the House to consider," Ruth observed while enjoying some fruit with her oatmeal. "Not just Representatives, but staff members as well. There are just too many suspects if we use gender to consider the writer of those letters. That's like going to market and looking for one grape fruit for breakfast when there are fifty in the bin."

"You're right," I nodded, while spreading jam on my toast. "I believe we will need to take a different approach. Maybe we should start small, perhaps with her office and then the other offices in her hall. Perhaps we should think about the faces she sees every day."

"You mean Representative Hash's staff?" Ruth asked, sipping her coffee.

"To start," I nodded, glancing at the morning paper. "Then we could look at the people in the offices in her hallway. Faces that she might see from week to week."

"That sounds like a lot of people to consider," Ruth observed.

"You're right," I sighed, being well aware of how many staffers pass in and out of an office during a typical week in the House. "Well…maybe we should go right to the source."

"You mean…Lana's granddaughter?" Ruth asked.

"Yes." I nodded and I reached over and took a sip of Ruth's coffee, which she doesn't mind me doing most mornings. "I think we need to get some time alone with her."

"Now *that* would be a simpler approach," Ruth nodded while enjoying taking a scoop of her oatmeal. "You know the direct approach is always my favorite."

"Yes, subtle is not in your vocabulary," I smiled while taking a few bites of my toast. "When I look back on this whole situation, Ruth, it seems to me that we've been talking more to Lana than Megan. I think it's about time we actually get a chance to have a private chat with the granddaughter to see what she thinks. We simply need to get her in a place where Lana is not around."

"So we don't need to speak with Lana anymore?" Ruth asked.

"I don't think so," I replied.

"Good," Ruth mumbled, glancing down at her coffee mug. "I don't like her. She's as bitter as my coffee."

"She is that," I sighed.

"Well, if we want to talk to Megan we certainly can't go back to Lana's house," Ruth sighed. "She'd stay between us and Megan the whole time."

"I don't even think Lana would let us in the front door," Ruth observed. "She made it perfectly clear that we're not *important* enough to warrant her attention."

"You're right," I replied while taking another bite of my toast. I was amazed at how quickly Ruth had picked up on Lana's true nature. "That's Lana being Lana, in my opinion. The granddaughter might be the same way. Normally, I'd suggest we talk to some of the well-connected socialites we know, but Megan is new to the city. She's only an intern, and really not known by the social circles we travel in. That's a problem for us."

"What about her work?" Ruth asked. "Could we swing by the office where she works and talk to her?"

"Perhaps," I nodded. "The only problem is that there are too many prying ears in an office. At least that was my experience when I worked there."

"Well...what do you suggest?" Ruth asked.

I didn't really have an answer. My thoughts went back to my days of working as a secretary in the office of a Representative. Other than leaving my desk for lunch or an occasional meeting, there were very few times when I was alone. Even working in the office at my desk, there were always people passing through and there were always phone calls to be taken. Then I recalled something that I was required to do when I first got hired. It was a task that no one in the office wanted to do, which is why it was always given to the lowest ranked person in the office. It was also a job that I did by myself. The mere recollection of this lowly task led me to think of a plan to get Megan alone. It wasn't the most clever plan I'd come up with, but I believed it would give us time to speak with Megan in a private way.

"Sister," I began, grinning at Ruth. "How would you feel if we changed our residence and became citizens of New Jersey?"

"I'm too old to move," Ruth grunted, finishing her oatmeal.

"I'm not talking about packing our suitcases," I grinned before finishing off my toast. "You see...I believe that being from New Jersey might be an advantage to us."

"I still don't know what you're talking about," Ruth grumbled.

I leaned across the breakfast table to Ruth and together we hatched a plan for how we could have a private conversation with Lana's granddaughter. The only thing that it would require from us would be a little white lie and, perhaps, a New Jersey accent.

## Chapter 16: WALK AND TALK

When visiting the House of Representatives, the sound of shoes smacking against marble floor always makes me smile. It's a familiar sound that brings back fond memories of my youth. I can still see myself walking down the long hallways, at the same important pace, going to or from meetings with my boss. I had that energetic stride and sense of importance about what I was doing. I got to meet interesting people and enjoy feeling like I was changing the world. Of course, barely in my twenties, I felt a sense of importance about everything I did in my life.

My sister and I were back in the Capital Building having our bags checked by security before walking through the long marble halls that spread out before us. My eyes scanned the white walls that ran on either side of the hallway before focusing on the plaques fixed next to each office door. We glanced at the names on the plaques, searching for one particular name. Soon we came to the plaque and name we were searching for.

"Here is Representative Tempest Hash's office," I announced.

"Good," Ruth replied and she turned and looked left then right. "I thought we were lost for a minute there. All of these hallways look the same to me. It really makes it difficult for someone to find their Representative's office. I don't know how you found your way around here, sister."

"When I started working here," I recalled, "I got lost more than once for the first few weeks. I guess since I was the youngest in the office, I was always being sent to an office to deliver files or pick them up. The more errands I was sent on the better I got at knowing my way around."

"Well," Ruth said, turning to the door, "I wonder how well Megan knows her way around."

"I hope she's working today," I mumbled.

"Let's go inside and find out," Ruth replied.

When Ruth grabbed the door handle and began to crack the door open, I placed my hand on her shoulder.

"Remember to try to talk with an accent when you speak," I whispered in her ear.

"I'm too old to begin acting," Ruth grumbled before swinging the door wide open.

Together we entered the office of Representative Hash. The moment we opened the door and stepped inside, I saw a tall woman with dark hair tied in a bun, wearing a navy blue dress, leaning over a desk with a young lady who looked like Lana's granddaughter. The tall woman stood up, turned to us, and quickly removed a pair of reading glasses that was sliding down her nose.

"Good afternoon," she smiled.

"Hello," I replied. "My name is Charlotte....Cullen. This is my sister Ruth Cullen. We're here to see Representative Hash."

"That would be me," she smiled.

"You look much younger in person," I grinned. "The photos in the newspaper don't do you justice."

"That's very sweet," Representative Hash laughed. "It's so nice of you two ladies to come all the way down here to see us. My staff tells me you're visiting here from Trenton, New Jersey?"

The expression on her face and the sweet tone in her words and the ready smile, was like a weather barometer was telling me she was in the midst of a re-election.

"That's right. I spoke with someone from your office about getting a tour of this massive building," I stated with the best New Jersey accent I could muster. I looked over at Ruth who started to laugh. My eyes turned back to Representative Hash and I smiled. "This building is so…huge! My sister and I were lucky to find your office."

"I'm glad you found us," she answered and she reached over and shook both of our hands. "It was so nice of you to call our office. It's good to see our constituents when they visit Washington. I have a very capable intern named Megan Granger who will be more than happy to give you a tour of the building."

I watched Representative Hash turn and look at a person by the filing cabinet. The person's back was to us, her head looking in an open drawer. Her long blond hair was all I needed to see. Suddenly the drawer to the cabinet closed and the person stood straight up and turned to us. It was Megan Granger.

"Megan," Representative Hash began, "could you take these ladies out and show them the nicer parts of the House. They're visiting from New Jersey so make it a memorable tour."

"Yes, ma'am," Megan said, but when she looked at me the expression on her face told me she was at first confused then skeptical of her assignment. She pointed to us. "Are you sure you want me to show them around?"

"You'll do fine, Megan. I have every confidence in you. Besides, I'm stuck in meetings all morning," Representative Hash explained. "I'll need the staff with me. Don't worry; you know your way around. Ladies, I do hope you have a wonderful stay in Washington and enjoy Megan's company this morning."

With those final words, Representative Hash dashed out of the office with two members of her staff in tow. Megan, Ruth and I were the only ones left in the room. Megan remained by the filing cabinet. Her eyes turned to us and the expression on her face told me she was harboring some suspicions about our story.

"I know you two," she said and her eyes narrowed. "I know that you're not visiting from New Jersey. Grandma told me about you both the day you came to visit our house with that cat."

"So did your grandmother tell you about all of the wonderful experiences she and I had working in these very same hallways?" I asked with a big smile.

"She said you were two busy bodies who stick your noses in other people's business," Megan replied with a face as rigid as a poker player.

After hearing those words, I could sense Lana's voice and spirit in what Megan said and how she looked. I could also see the expressionless face with the perfect complexion. I could hear the direct tone and see those piercing blue eyes. Perhaps it was because we were back in the Capitol Building, but I could feel Megan's words and appearance press some emotional buttons deep inside of me. Buttons that her grandmother had pressed years earlier. I breathed in and tried to cool my simmering blood. I looked at the young girl who had simply given voice to her grandmother's thoughts and forced a smile out of my cheeks.

"Your grandmother is prone to being a bit...dramatic," I said with a very delicate tone of voice. "When you know someone as long as I've known her...one learns to take her harsh words with a grain of salt."

"Well," Megan sighed, standing up from behind her desk, "since you worked here, Miss Dupree, you probably know your way around here better than I do.

I'm still getting lost when I'm asked to deliver something to another Representative. Maybe you should give me a tour?"

"Of course," I nodded. "There are little things to notice around this place. Tricks I used to get around. If you know what to look for...you'll get better at walking around here, too."

"Show me what you mean," Megan suggested. "What tricks and things are you talking about?"

"Follow me and let me show you," I grinned, gesturing to the door.

In an odd sort of way, I had won Megan's trust by telling her I would help her negotiate the massive hallways of the House. This simple promise told me that she was willing to listen to my suggestions and ready to trust my advice. So far my plan was working.

It had been a long time since I'd taken a stroll around the halls of the Capitol Building. Since the day I left, there was never a need for me to return. As the years slipped by, elections came and went and the people I once worked with were either voted out or retired. The lucky few to remain simply died in office.

So by touring the capital on this particular morning, it brought back good memories to see the corridors, watch how the people still moved at a brisk pace, and how they still carried themselves with that same self-important posture. There was simply a sense of urgency about most of the people Megan led us by. While some things about the interior of the building had changed, the people working here still looked and acted the same. The exceptions to this were the occasional tourists we saw strolling aimlessly around. There was no sense of urgency about them. They took their time, strolled around and took pictures of every detail.

"So, Megan," Ruth began, "do you like working here?"

"Very much," she replied, leading us down one hall.

"Are you looking for a career in politics?" Ruth pressed.

"I want to make a difference for people," Megan replied and for the first time I saw the slightest of smiles appear on her face. "There are a lot of poor and hungry people in this country. I think the best way to help them will be by working here."

I had to smile myself when I heard those youthful idealistic words of hope in reference to working for our government. Sad to say that, in my opinion, a few years on the job should be enough to knock some of the luster off of Megan's hopes.

While I listened to Megan share her aspirations it struck me how different she sounded from Lana. While they resembled one another in appearance and tone of voice, there was a clear difference in priorities between the two women at around the same age. In all the years I'd known Lana, I'd never heard her talk about helping others through her work. From what I remember, Lana was only content to help herself.

Eventually we found ourselves standing under a signature stop for anyone visiting the Capitol Building. The massive rotunda to the Capitol was a work of art that never failed to lure a tourist's eye. Even though she'd been an intern for weeks, Megan still stopped and looked up at the elaborate painting on the interior of the dome. While I had seen it many times, I also stopped and looked up. The dome was fixed so high above us which made it hard to appreciate the level of detail. I always thought it a shame to have such a masterpiece so far from view.

"That is my favorite part of the building," Megan said, looking up like one of the tourists. "Sometimes I'll come here over my lunch, sit down and just look up at that portrait. Someone in the office told me it was painted by an Italian artist. They even say that at the center of the painting is George Washington seated in the clouds. I think the woman sitting next to him must be Martha Washington."

"Actually, that's a common mistake," I said, pointing up. "The woman to his right isn't Mrs. Washington. In fact, it's actually the Goddess of Liberty. I can understand your thinking, though. She does bear a striking resemblance to Martha Washington."

"A powerful woman is behind every powerful man," Ruth spoke up. "Don't you agree, Megan?"

"I'd suppose," Megan replied.

"So what great man are you behind?" Ruth asked.

"What?" Megan asked, her head dipping down to look at Ruth.

"She asked what great man you're behind?" I said, repeating the question and stepping closer to her.

"Representative Hash is a great woman," she mumbled. "That's all I know. Why…why are you asking me this question?"

"Because there is a man in your life," Ruth pressed.

"What do you mean?" Megan said, looking confused by the course of our conversation.

"Are you dating anyone?" I asked.

"No," Megan softly answered. "Why would you ask me such a thing? That's none of your business!"

"Because of this," I finally said, handing Megan one of the envelopes we collected from Lana's house.

"What is this?" she asked, turning the envelope in her hand.

"We believe this is a letter from your lover," I replied.

Megan's mouth dropped open and she pulled the letter out of the envelope. Her eyes darted from side to side as she read the words and her face turned red as a rose.

"How...how did you get this?" Megan hissed, her eyebrows pushing together.

"I'd rather not say," I replied. "I'll tell you this much, Megan. Having known your grandmother as I long as I have, I watched her go down this path many times when she was your age. Finding an older man to love. I can tell you it never ended happily for her and it won't end happily for you either."

I paused for a moment and looked at Megan. I was clearly aware that she thought of me as some old nosey person giving her advice. It would be all too easy for her to dismiss my words. I knew I needed to give her a bit of a nudge to get her to confess to me. My mind was racing and then I thought of the perfect thing to say.

"I know who wrote that letter," I fibbed and I kept a straight face while I did it. "You live in this town as long as we have—it only took me a few phone calls to get a name. What do you think his wife and children would make of you?"

"How did you ..." Megan stammered and her face went from red to maroon.

"There are no secrets in Washington!" Ruth snapped. "If you're going to work in Washington your grandmother should have told you that rule."

"Consider that your first lesson about this town," I added.

"Please don't tell my grandmother," Megan replied, her eyes growing wide. "He told me it was just him and his wife. He didn't mention having children."

"Married men are never honest with their lovers," Ruth sighed.

"Oh, Gerald," Megan whispered, looking down at the floor.

Ruth looked at me and her eyebrows when up for about a second. We had a first name. "Well, I hope this experience doesn't make it awkward for you at work," I observed. "Romances in the work place do tend to make things uncomfortable for everyone."

"He said he loved me," Megan mumbled and she quickly pulled up her phone and began texting wildly. I managed to stroll around her and peak at the name on the screen. *G. Wilkens* was the name I saw.

"Thank you," I whispered while Megan texted her heart out to her lover.

I quickly turned and walked away with Ruth trailing behind me.

"Do you know who she's talking about?" Ruth asked me.

"I don't," I replied, "but I can ask the receptionist we walked by on the way in the building. She might be able to tell us how to find him. The name we're looking for is Gerald Wilkens."

Together we moved down the long hallways, up a set of steps, then found ourselves back at the main entrance. I was impressed that my memory was good enough to find my way around the Capital Building without any wrong turns. When we arrived at the main entrance, a nice young man was seated at a large round desk. He looked at us and I summoned my sweetest smile.

"My sister and I are here to see Representative Gerald Wilkens," I stated.

"One moment please," the young man said and he began typing quite furiously on a keyboard. When he finished staring at the screen he looked up at both of us and smiled.

"Representative Wilkens is located in the Rayburn Office Building," he stated.

"And who does he represent?" I asked.

"The Thirteenth District of New Jersey," the man quietly stated. "Would you like directions to his office?"

"I think we can find him," I answered.

When we finished, I turned and led Ruth out the door of the Capitol Building. I couldn't help but pause when I left. I turned around, smiled at the building the way one would smile at an old friend. I led Ruth down a set of steps and headed for the street.

"Where are we going?" Ruth asked. "The Rayburn Building is back there."

"We need another letter," I explained while waving for a cab. "If we're going to confront a Representative about having an affair with an intern, we'll need more than our word on the matter. We'll need some proof, too."

## Chapter 17:  THE SIGNATURE MOMENT

Since Megan had kept the letter I confronted her
with, I needed another one. Ruth and I were fortunate
enough to get a taxi and head home. We were also
fortunate that the traffic was agreeable enough that we
were able to get home, grab another letter and ride back
to the Capitol Building in a short amount of time.

During the cab ride I took the liberty of calling
Representative Wilken's office to get a sense for his
schedule. Of course, they simply told me that he'd be in
and out of the office during the day because of
meetings. Having worked in the House for a
Representative, I found this to be a perfectly legitimate
claim. With that in mind, I spent the rest of our ride
back to the Capital Building thinking of a way to lure
him out of a meeting.

Soon we arrived at Representative Wilkens' office.
His secretary, who introduced himself as Shawn,
explained that his boss was out of the office and in a
committee meeting. The meeting he was attending was
scheduled to finish in a half hour, so Ruth and I decided
to stay for the balance of time.

Now if you've ever been to the office of a
Representative, especially a newly elected one, then
you know that the offices aren't very big. I took a few
steps around the room once or twice, pointing out a
picture to Ruth. It was a photograph of Representative
Wilkens shaking hands with the newly-elected
President.

"Representative Wilkens has friends in high places," Ruth observed.

"The beauty of campaigns," I replied. "Everyone appears to be important when they get a picture with a President."

We stood silent staring at the photo. Then Ruth leaned in close to me.

"He doesn't look like the philandering type," Ruth whispered.

"They never do," I whispered back.

While I was expecting Megan to be involved with a man who was handsome or dashing, Representative Wilkens appeared to be neither in the photo we looked at. His dark hair, while combed to the side, tended to stick straight up on the top of his head. Also, I thought his eyes appeared wider than normal, like he was surprised to be having his picture taken. He was taller than the President, with a lean frame that caused me to guess he must exercise or had a good metabolism.

After a review of various ornaments around the office and the pictures scattered around the walls, Ruth and I finally settled into a small leather couch. Time slowly ticked by as we watched Shawn answer the phone a few times in between doing some paperwork and poking at his smartphone. My eyes kept drifting between Shawn and the clock on the wall behind his desk. When I saw the half hour was up, and Representative Wilkens hadn't returned from his meeting, my mind began to grow restless and my patience began to wane.

"How long should we dangle here like a couple of worms?" Ruth whispered.

"I think we've waited long enough," I whispered back and I began to drum my fingers on my knee. "Since we made the effort to come here to see him, perhaps it's time for the good Representative to seek us out."

"And how do you propose we lure a U.S. Representative to our quiet little home?" Ruth asked.

Glancing at Ruth, I drew in my breath and stood up.

"Do you have an envelope, Shawn?" I asked, stepping in front of the secretary's desk. "I have something I'd like to leave for Representative Wilkens."

When Shawn handed me a legal envelope, I slipped one of Lana's naughty letters inside and licked the envelope shut. Then I borrowed one of Shawn's pens, placed the envelope firmly on his desk, and wrote a message that I thought would get his boss's attention:

*Dear Representative Wilkens,*
*I have more of these letters in my possession. Please contact me at the following number so we can talk.*
*Charlotte Dupree*

Underneath the message I wrote our phone number, handed the envelope to Shawn and quietly left the office.

Deep down inside, I had a sneaking suspicion that the envelope might get lost on Shawn's cluttered desk. I also wondered if Representative Wilkens might be too busy to even check the contents of the envelope.

Both questions were answered later that evening when the phone rang right when we were sitting down to eat a lovely casserole that my sister had made for dinner. After a brief introduction from Representative Wilkens, we agreed to meet with him at Lafayette Square. While we regretted departing the house, and the lovely aroma coming from the casserole, his prompt reply to our message told me he was, in my opinion, nervous about what I'd sent him. The fact that he wanted to meet so soon told me he was desperate.

We each took a few bites of dinner, fed Mezzo and Oliver, then grabbed our coats. An orange evening sky greeted us as we stepped out the front door and followed the sidewalk from our home to Lafayette Square. We found an empty park bench to sit down where we looked around at the smattering of people taking an evening stroll. We even discussed the appearance of a few young people while we waited for Representative Wilkens to arrive.

As the moments ticked by, we watched the sky turn from peach, to red, to violet. Then, walking up from the far end of the park, I spotted a man in a long dark overcoat approach. His steps were fast and heading in our direction. The closer he got the more I recognized the unkempt hair on the top of his head. When he walked up to us I could see his eyes get wider when he looked at us. By the time he reached our bench, I managed to smile and in the calmest voice I could muster said, "Thank you for coming, Representative Wilkens. I believe we have much to talk about."

Chapter 17:  THE LITTLE SECRET

Representative Wilkens wore dark framed glasses that he nervously pushed up the slope of his nose before blinking twice. There was no courteous smile or polite chit chat to begin our discourse, which I must admit I found refreshing from a politician. Instead of a photo-op smile or a handshake, Representative Wilkens simply wore a scowl on his lips. His hands were tucked in his coat pockets and his dark eyes narrowed into slits when he sized us up.

"Are you ladies responsible for the envelope left in my office?" he asked in a demanding tone of voice.

"We are," I replied as calmly as I could.

He paused for a moment, looked around the park, then took one step closer to us.

"What do you think you're doing?" he asked and his head tipped to one side.

"I should ask you the same question," I finally spoke up and I pointed at him before making my points. "I worked in the House for a good many years. I know shenanigans like the kind you're up to happen on occasion. I remember how some Representatives see a staff of interns as a dessert cart to devour whenever the mood strikes. That's how I see you."

"I beg your pardon!" Representative Wilkens snapped, his glasses slipping down his nose a bit. "You have no basis for making that kind of statement. Do you even have proof?"

"You wrote that letter I left in your office," I pointed out. "That's why you're here. I'm not telling you something you don't already know, Representative Wilkens."

"You make this kind of accusation in front of my wife and you'll have a lawyer knocking on your front door," he warned, pointing at Ruth and me.

I paused for a moment to consider if he was bluffing or not. I turned to Ruth, who I knew would be even more direct with her words than I was with mine. I smiled at my sister and nodded my head once for her to speak.

"You see, it's not just the affair that concerns us," Ruth began. "I mean my sister and I have grown up in this town. We're quite accustomed to the occasional rumor about an affair involving a politician."

"I'm afraid you're chasing the wrong fox, ladies," he replied, looking out on the garden fixed across from the bench. "There was no affair and I'll destroy that letter you gave me to substantiate my claim on this matter."

"Let me be very clear about something," I said, making the tone of my voice a little sharper. "I have more letters that you wrote to Megan. While in your office waiting for a half hour, I also managed to snatch this small note from the desk of your receptionist. I'm quite good at matching handwriting styles and when I saw the way you wrote certain letters in that note to Shawn, and I compared that note to the words in your letter to Megan—well—it was hard to miss the similarities. That, combined with the fact that you're here, tells me I'm chasing the *right* fox."

Representative Wilkens turned his gaze up from us and scanned the park. He tucked his hands in his coat pockets and looked back to me.

"Where did you get those letters?" he snapped.

"None of your concern," I replied. "Now are you ready to talk about your affair with Megan or should I take my evidence to the police?"

"It's not a crime to have an affair," he said with a matter of fact tone of voice.

"It is when a dead body is involved," Ruth spoke up.

The comment drew a startled look from Representative Wilkens. He pulled one hand out of his coat pocket, ran it across the top of his head and began to pace back and forth in front of us.

"What are you talking about?" he asked in a more discreet tone.

"There was a young woman killed in the home where Megan was living," I began to explain. "Could it be that someone was feeling jealous about your shenanigans? Jealous enough to kill someone they thought was Megan?"

"Perhaps your wife?" Ruth suggested.

"My wife?" he asked and he stopped pacing and looked directly at us. "My wife is the best person I know. To sit there and imply that she...would kill someone...you just don't know her very well to make that assumption."

"Why were you writing those letters?" I asked.

"Megan and I couldn't communicate with each other by cell phone or email," he explained. "I mean look what happened to Hillary Clinton with her email scandal. Nothing is secure online. So I came up with the idea of writing to Megan. She told me to address my letters to her grandmother and Megan said she'd intercept them."

"Perhaps your wife spotted the address on one of your envelopes," Ruth suggested.

"Yes," I nodded, "and then she went to the house and attacked someone she thought was Megan. From what we learned, the maid was about the same age as Megan. They were about the same height, too. It would be very easy for anyone not thinking straight to walk into a house and hurt the first young girl they saw in a fit of rage."

"You can't prove that," he mumbled. "It's reckless to even say something like that in this town."

"If I talk to your wife, I suspect I'll get to the core of the matter," I replied, feeling quite confident in my assumptions.

"Call the police," Representative Wilkins suggested. "Tell them what you think. If they wish to pursue it then I'll help. Neither my wife nor I are murderers."

He checked his watch and looked at us with an expression that told me he had somewhere else to be.

"Are we done?" he asked. "Is there anything else you wish to say?"

"You're about to start a re-election bid...aren't you?" I asked.

"I don't know yet," he sighed. "That's a conversation I need to have with my wife before deciding."

"Do you really want your local newspapers covering an investigation for a murder...even if you didn't kill anyone?" I asked.

Representative Wilkens turned and looked at us both.

"Is this blackmail? Do you want money?" he asked.

"Money isn't the issue," I laughed.

"Then what do you want?" he asked.

"We would simply like to talk to your wife. Perhaps the four of us could enjoy a lovely dinner some evening," Ruth said.

"We don't need favors or money from you," I quickly added. "A night out with you and your wife is what we want."

Representative Wilkens said nothing to the invitation.

"I'm quite certain it would be an uncomfortable evening for you," I smiled. "My sister and I would like to know who killed that lovely young maid. Now if you want your affair to stay out of the newspapers, wait for our call and we will give you a date and time to meet with us. My sister and I are very familiar with the best restaurants in Washington. I promise you whatever restaurant we pick it will be a quality establishment for you and your wife."

Wilkens looked at us both, shook his head and simply walked away in silence.

"Was that a yes or a no?" Ruth asked.

"I suppose we'll find out when we call him," I replied.

With the sky turning from violet to black, we quickly headed home. With streetlights glowing and headlights flickering through the streets, we quietly did the short walk back to our house, discussing the words of Representative Wilkens with each step.

Chapter 18: DISCRETION AND DINNER

Of all the restaurants in the D.C. area that we frequent, the Occidental Grill holds a special place in our hearts. Located not far from the White House, it has sat along Pennsylvania Avenue since 1906. As anyone who goes there knows, the restaurant likes to fill its walls with photographs of all the famous people who have eaten there. On those occasions when Ruth and I stop into the Occidental Grill for dinner, our eyes are always drawn to the famous faces framed next to our table.

The smiling faces of Presidents Teddy Roosevelt, Calvin Coolidge, Franklin Roosevelt and John F. Kennedy are among the many historical figures who have dined at the Occidental. Even photos of Amelia Earhart and Winston Churchill catch my eye whenever we dine. What Ruth and I like about the restaurant, aside from the history of its famous customers, is their extensive selection of seafood entrees. In addition to their good food, we also enjoy the discretion that the restaurant is known for. Given the factors surrounding this meal, discretion was our primary reason for choosing the Occidental.

Stepping through the main entrance, one is greeted by a large dining area with exposed wood beams overhead, sage-colored walls and high-back wooden chairs pushed into tables covered with white linens. This night, most of the seats were taken and voices filled the air. Along the walls, the usual black and white photos of celebrities and historical figures filled every inch, grinning in approval at the scene.

When we arrived, the hostess greeted us and we explained that we had made reservations for a more private section of the restaurant to eat. She checked her notes, grabbed four menus and led us through the main room and into a side room known as the Presidential Room. Bright finished wood walls lined this intimate dining area. Painted portraits of former Presidents were framed and hung on the walls. The hostess handed us menus and told us a waitress would be by soon.

"Do you think he'll come?" Ruth whispered.

"I left a message with his office," I replied. "If he knows what's good for him, he'll join us."

For the next few minutes, Ruth and I sat, reviewed the menu, chatted with the waitress and waited for our guests. We nibbled on some dinner rolls. We scanned the room and chatted about the presidential portraits on display. We also discussed a photo of former Washington football coach George Allen that I spotted back in the main dining room. This prompted a frequent debate between myself and Ruth over who the better coach was. As die-hard fans, it doesn't take much for us to talk about the state of football in Washington. We began to dig in and I made some fine points about Coach Allen when the tall lean frame of Representative Wilkens entered the room. Much to my surprise, his wife was not beside him.

"Where is Mrs. Wilkens?" I asked as he settled himself into a chair at our table.

"My wife will not be joining us," he stated in a direct tone of voice. "She knows nothing and I would prefer to keep it that way."

I looked at Ruth and the expression on her face made me think she believed him.

"Well," I began, "I'd suppose a good place to start would be to ask who does know about this? Is there anyone in your office who knew about your affair?"

"About what?" he asked.

"Your affair with Megan Granger," I replied.

He grabbed a dinner roll, tore it in half and stuck one piece into his mouth.

"Royce White," Wilkins answered while he chewed the bread. "He's my chief of staff. I talk to him more than my wife from one day to the next. The other person who knew was the maid you mentioned. The one who died."

"Really?" Ruth asked, sitting forward and leaning her elbows on the table.

"So how did the maid find out about you and Megan?" I asked.

"The same way you did," Representative Wilkens sighed, before taking another bite of his roll. "You see, we thought it would be so easy to communicate by handwritten letters. Of course, we would see each other in the office, too. I guess she was careless with where she kept my letters. From what I gather, the maid was cleaning Megan's room when she found one of them. She confronted Megan about it. Needless to say, I was surprised when I received a letter from this...Maria Nunez. She told me what she knew and asked me for money to keep her from going to the press."

That statement took both Ruth's and my breath away. I could feel my body lean forward and my elbows went firmly on the table. My good manners were completely overridden by my curiosity.

"The maid was blackmailing you?" Ruth asked.

"Yes, she was," he replied before sipping some water.

"My gosh," I sighed, glancing across the table at Ruth. "Well, I guess you're quite happy with how things played out. Given what happened to Maria, it saved you some money and embarrassing press coverage."

"Unless," he said and he waved a finger across the table at Ruth and me. "Unless you two are looking to do the same thing."

"As I told you before…we're not here to blackmail you," I said.

"Blackmail?" Ruth laughed. "I can assure you that we're both well off, Mr. Wilkens. You don't have to worry about us asking for money from you or anyone else."

I watched as he nodded to both of us before reaching for another roll.

"So back to my original question," I began, sitting back in my seat. "How many people knew about your affair? Was it just your chief of staff?"

"Maria, Megan and Royce," Wilkens nodded. "Now if one of them began to tell other people about what was happening, that would have been out of my control."

"You mean if the killer found out?" Ruth asked.

"Exactly," he nodded back.

"So…if the killer found out…then perhaps it might have been someone who was sympathetic towards you," Ruth observed.

"That's a possibility," I nodded and I gestured to Representative Wilkens with my hand. "Although, with all due respect, I must admit I'd find it hard to feel any sympathy for a man who chooses to romance a young girl in college."

"A girl young enough to be his daughter," Ruth added.

Representative Wilkens said nothing. He simply sat with his eyes fixed to the table. He took a bite from his roll and seemed content to remain silent. He put the roll down on his plate, looked at Ruth and me and cleared his throat.

"Are either of you married?" he finally asked.

"No," I quickly replied.

"Then you don't know what it's like to find the love of your life only to lose that love because of age, time and other commitments," he began. "You see, ladies, you get to a certain age when you can start to sense the passion wane. Instead of love being something like a bright, bold and beautiful garden in the spring it becomes more like stagnant dark flowers in late fall. That's what my marriage looked like to me. That's when I decided not to stand by and do nothing. I decided to pursue that romantic passion all over again. To experience young love at my age is a blessing. The passion that a young woman brings to my life is the spark I needed. Megan has changed my life for the better."

I looked at Ruth. I could tell by her expression that neither one of us was going to feel sympathetic for this louse. Yes, he was a politician who was good with words and phrases but in the final analysis, he was wrong for what he did. The fact that he didn't even apologize for his actions told me something about how self-absorbed he was.

"This…young love…is it also a blessing for your wife?" Ruth asked.

The words led him to tap his one finger on the edge of the table.

"I still care about her and don't want her hurt," Wilkens replied. "Please don't go to the press with this. My wife and I…we need to sit down and have a conversation about our marriage. I understand that."

"Frankly, I don't care about your marriage," I said and I looked around at a couple entering the Presidential Room. The hostess sat them at a table on the other side of the room and I gave her a dissatisfied look. I leaned forward in my seat and tried to speak at a whisper. "Someone lost their life over your indiscretion, Mr. Wilken. Now the police may or may not want to investigate but I would like to learn more about what happened. Aren't you the least bit curious?"

I glanced across the room at the party of four seated at another table. I could see them picking up their menus and speaking in normal tones of voice. Seeing how preoccupied they were made it a little easier for me to speak in a normal tone of voice.

"This is an election year," he quickly replied with a soft tone. "I can't afford to be curious about a murder during an election year."

"Fortunately for you, we *can* afford to be," Ruth quickly replied.

With those words, the Representative looked at both of us and stood up.

"Aren't you going to order?" Ruth asked.

"I've lost my appetite," Wilkens said before walking away.

I grabbed a menu and began to look at the choices for what to order. I glanced over to see Ruth doing the same. While the entrees I was reviewing looked quite good, I kept thinking about what he'd told us in that short conversation.

"Do you believe him?" I heard Ruth ask from behind her menu.

"I know you're always quoting presidents to me, Ruth, but this just popped into my head when I was listening to Representative Wilkens," I explained, grabbing the last dinner roll from our basket. "Thomas Jefferson once said, 'When a man assumes a public trust he should consider himself a public property.' I think Representative Wilkens has forgotten President Jefferson's words. I think he's forgotten about the public and is only concerned with himself. Yes, I do believe he's acting on his own lust and his own interests. Did his lust for Megan cause him to kill Maria…I don't know."

With those final words, the waitress came and we ordered. While I had the crab cakes, Ruth decided to be adventurous and order the Norwegian Halibut. With a small candle flickering between us, we enjoyed our food, chatted about some gossip and took in the atmosphere. Soon more patrons arrived and filled the other table around us. Their voices began to fill the Presidential Room. Yet, while the atmosphere became more festive, our words held a different tone. While loud voices and laughter rose up around us from time to time, our voices remained soft, our words measured, and our dialogue centered on the good Representative from New Jersey and his carefully chosen words.

## Chapter 19:  PERSPECTIVE

Growing up in Washington D.C. provided Ruth and me with plenty of opportunities to appreciate art. In fact, when we were young girls our mother started taking us to art galleries at an early age. Ruth and I knew names like Monet and Rembrandt long before we ever heard of Mother Goose or Peter Rabbit. From our many trips to galleries, our mother instilled in us a true appreciation for art. She also instilled in us the value of perspective.

When we'd stand in front of a painting or a sculpture, mother would always tell us to never consider a piece of art by simply standing in one spot. She taught us to understand the importance of considering it from many perspectives. Sometimes she would gently take our hands and move us a few steps to the right, or a few steps to the left, or move us closer or farther back. When she did this, the art we were looking at seemed to change. In short, our mother taught us how perspective can alter the way something looks. How it can illuminate something or add a layer of darkness to it. For a pair of young girls, this lesson seemed a bit silly, but in the long run it taught Ruth and me how important perspective can be, not just in our appreciation of art, but in life, too. I was reminded of this lesson when I thought of Representative Wilkens.

Since hearing his name, Ruth and I had only one perspective of this philandering Representative from New Jersey. Our picture of Gerald Wilkens came directly from his indiscretion and the letters we had in our possession. Of course, it would be easy to simply paint him as a scoundrel and leave it at that. However, Ruth and I knew there had to be more to the man that we didn't see. We also knew it would be a challenge to learn more.

As lifelong residents of Washington, we know there is a pecking order to politicians. It's easy to be knowledgeable about a president or maybe a few senators. However, it's downright impossible to be aware of the habits and interests of every state Representative in town. If you go by the numbers, there are simply too many members in the House of Representatives to keep tabs on. That's why I thought it was important for us to do a little digging. We needed to learn more about Representative Wilkens from the people who knew him best.

After some discussions, Ruth and I decided on a plan to broaden our perspective. One morning we picked up the phone and sent a carefully worded invitation through the social networks of Washington. The message was quite clear to everyone we called. We were going to host a small tea in support of Representative Wilkens' re-election campaign. Anyone who was a supporter, or simply liked the man, was welcome to attend. My sister and I were curious to see who, if anyone, would accept our open-ended invitation.

When the date of our tea social arrived, Ruth and I counted ten people entering our home and filling our sitting room. We had ladies with white hair. Ladies with colored hair. A young lady and a young man who still had natural hair color and looked to be college age.

All in all, I think I can speak for my sister when I say we were quite surprised to see this kind of a range of support for a Representative who hadn't been in Washington for more than one term.

As was usually the case when hosting such an event, the conversations began by circling around the fringes of safe topics like the weather, the latest art collections to arrive in town, and what ballets were being performed. All topics that everyone enjoyed with equal measure. Yet, as the second hour began, the topics of discourse started to spiral into political waters, which brought out stronger opinions from our guests.

While the voices grew more heated, Ruth served some wonderful sandwiches with tea while one guest went on about Representative Wilkens' record on matters of supporting abortion clinics. Another pointed out his repeated efforts to cut defense spending. Yet another voiced concerns over his support to borrow from social security to fund other projects. I even heard one guest complain that Representative Wilkens crossed party lines too much. All in all, I heard very little to indicate he was making anyone happy.

As for his personal life, all of our guests said they'd heard nothing but good things about his wife. During his one term in office, Mrs. Wilkens had managed to spearhead a literacy effort for inner city children at a school in Washington D.C. The program was designed to offer help after school for students who were weak in reading. Mrs. Wilkens coordinated this idea with volunteers from a local chapter of a retirement agency. By all accounts, the program was a resounding success.

As I listened to the details, I couldn't help but admire Mrs. Wilkens. At least she made the effort to look around the city she and her husband had moved to in an attempt to find a need to meet. From everything that was said about her, my perspective on Mrs. Wilkens had grown to real admiration. As far as her relationship with her husband, no one could say for certain if the marriage was sound or not. The Wilkens were seen attending various functions around town and by all accounts they always appeared to be happy.

"She has a smile on her face when she's with him," one lady spoke up.

"A dog looks happy when it's led on a leash," Ruth blurted out at one point. Her comment drew a few giggles from our guests. "It doesn't mean it's happy with its owner, just that it's happy with its surroundings."

"Are you comparing Mrs. Wilkens to...a dog?" someone asked in a such a way that it brought a hush to the room.

Ruth cast a sour look at the question and cleared her throat.

"I'm merely stating that Charlotte and I have seen our share of politicians and their spouses over the years," Ruth explained. "There's little doubt that being the wife of a politician is challenging work. In my lifetime, I've seen many of them come to Washington in support of their husbands. Eventually, the wives I've known realize that their husbands were not elected to a job, but to a way of life. A way of life that, in my opinion, leaves very little time for family. I've seen many spouses get involved in other causes. Pretty soon they get so caught up in their cause or charity that they barely notice the husband, who is also consumed by his job. Pretty soon they become two bodies that simply pass in a big house in Georgetown. I wonder if that's the case with Mrs. Wilkens and her husband?"

No one spoke after this insight. No one even made eye contact with me.

"They have no family living with them," one woman finally spoke up. "At one party I overheard Mrs. Wilkens share her disdain for having to move to Washington to live with her husband. They have three children. All of them are grown and living back in New Jersey. From what I heard…she misses them terribly."

"Does she go back to see them?" I asked.

No one spoke, but it was a good working theory to say that when Mrs. Wilkens was back in New Jersey visiting her children, the husband was left in Washington to pursue Megan. He certainly wouldn't be the first politician in the history of Washington to cheat on his wife. However, it is rare that such an infidelity leads to a murder.

"And what about his chief of staff?" I asked. "A man named Royce White. Does anyone know anything about him?"

"You mean the Great White?" the young man in the group laughed. "That's what they call him."

"And why do they call him that?" Ruth asked.

"Because when there's blood in the political waters, the Great White has a reputation for striking without hesitation," the young man explained.

"So they named him after a shark?" another person nodded.

"I guess they have the same instincts," the young man replied.

"And how did Representative Wilkens meet…the Great White?" I asked.

"I heard he worked on Wilkens' campaign," one person stated.

"I read a few articles about Royce White," an older woman spoke up. "The article said that he was the first person Wilkens hired after the election. From the accounts I read, Mr. White is young…but he operates with great political savvy. One article I read cited how he carries himself like a seasoned politician."

"So, other than striking back at political rivals…what else does he do?" I asked.

"He isn't afraid to get his hands dirty," another woman spoke up. "He can take a political punch as easily as he throws one. At least that's what the reporter who wrote the piece I read had to say about him. He stands his ground on policies that are important to his party and he won't hesitate to tell Wilkens how to vote on a bill. Again, this is based on just the one article I read."

"So how loyal is he?" Ruth asked. "I mean…does he worship the ground Wilkens walks on or does he control Wilkens? Is White a fanatic or not so much?"

"What do you mean by…worship?" a young man asked.

"Sometimes people who support a politician will do so with blind loyalty," I clarified. "They'll do whatever they need to serve their candidate regardless of the law," Ruth explained.

To my right, I noticed another person, this time a young woman who looked all of twenty, raise her hand as if she were trying to ask a question in school.

"I saw Royce White being interviewed on TV," she began. "He said he's worked for two other Representatives and one Senator. So he sounds like he has some experience working in Washington."

"That's good to know," I nodded. "You see, someone who moves around that much can have a broader perspective of the political landscape. From what I understand, folks like White move from candidate to candidate with great regularity. I doubt he'd jeopardize his reputation by just following Wilken's orders."

"Is there anything else to learn about this…Great White?" Ruth asked.

"He's also a Christian," the young girl stated. "When I heard him interviewed on the radio once I liked how he spoke about his relationship with God. He's quite proud of it. He was raised in the Bible belt and can even quote scripture like a minister. The interviewer I heard let White explain how he and his wife have been outspoken about the sanctity of marriage. White even said he wants to pass legislation to make it harder to divorce. Can you imagine? White thinks young couples today just give up too easily on marriage."

"Interesting," I sighed, thinking back to Representative Wilkens' predicament with his wife.

"Yes," Ruth smiled. "I wonder if he broached that discussion with Representative Wilkens."

Soon the evening drew to a close. Once all the guests had left, I told Ruth the conversations I'd heard strengthened my desire to meet Mrs. Wilkens. We also talked some more about what we'd learned about the mysterious Royce White. We also talked about whether White's sentiments on marriage came about because of his faith or because of Representative Wilkens' upcoming election. Perhaps Mrs. Wilkens could shed some light on the re-election campaign that her husband was determined to undertake.

Chapter 19: A NIGHT AT THE THEATER

For those who live outside the Capital Beltway, Washington D.C. is primarily known as a city of politics and power. It's a perception that permeates our country. However, for those of us fortunate enough to call the nation's capital home, we citizens know all too well how much the arts mean to the city.

Walk a few blocks and one cannot help but notice the wide range of museums, theaters, and galleries scattered around town. Even more prominent are the buildings in Washington that feature classic architectural styles. Most anyone who lives in Washington, and is surrounded by such culture, eventually grows in their appreciation for it.

I was reminded of the importance that art has on our city when we were visiting Representative Wilkens. While waiting in his office, I overheard his secretary make a call to order a pair of tickets to a performance at the Kennedy Center. I made a special effort to remember the event, the time and the date for the tickets, as confirmed over the phone by the secretary. Knowing that Representative Wilkens and his wife were planning to go to the ballet together made it all the more imperative for me to recall these details for a chance to meet Mrs. Gerald Wilkens. With the date of the show close at hand, I decided to act on this information by calling for tickets.

Over the years, Ruth and I have been to the Kennedy Center for the Performing Arts many times. We first started going to performances as young ladies back in

1971. As a matter of fact, we were in attendance for one of the first operas to be performed there, *Beatrix Cencil*. While we found the music quite moving, the storyline of a daughter paying assassins to kill her abusive father was nothing we could relate to. The fact that the daughter dies in the end gave Ruth and me much to discuss when we got home.

As anyone familiar with the Kennedy Center knows, the building houses six different theaters for performances. After placing a few phone calls, I learned that the ballet that Senator Wilkens would be attending was in the Eisenhower Theater, named after the former President who initially funded the construction of the center. Over a thousand people can attend performances in the Eisenhower Theater. Having gone to a few performances in this particular theater, Ruth and I knew it was not as large as some of the other venues at the Kennedy Center. So after some discussion, we decided to buy two tickets in hopes of finding Representative Wilkens and his wife.

The night we arrived for the ballet, I was struck by how different the inside of the theater looked from when we were there last. I read somewhere that the theater had been refurbished some time ago. The last time we were in the Eisenhower Theater, the walls and ceiling were dark wood and the carpeting and seats were ruby red. Now the theater was much brighter in appearance. A light ashen rug, light wood paneling on the walls and tan seating gave the theater a more pleasant look, in my opinion. Once we finished commenting on the decor, Ruth and I turned our attention to the number of people in attendance and looked around at the hundreds of well-dressed men and women seated and waiting for the performance to begin.

"Look at all the faces," I heard Ruth say.

"It looks like a full house," I nodded, scanning the audience.

"This is going to be impossible, Charlotte," Ruth grumbled and she pointed around at the rows of seats and the balcony fixed above us. "So many faces; how will you know where to look for Representative Wilkens and his wife?"

"Let's think this through," I smiled at my sister. "You and I have been here for the ballet before. We know where Members of Congress and their spouses like to sit. For a ballet, they always prefer the lower middle section, not up high and not in the balcony of the theater. Everyone who knows anything about this theater will tell you the same thing. I would imagine that Representative Wilkens's wife would like nothing more from her husband than the best. I would also imagine that it eases his conscience to obey her wishes, given his philandering ways. Therefore, you and I should ignore the balcony and take a slow walk down the aisles of the front sections of the theater. You check one side and I'll check the other. If either one of us spots Representative Wilkens wave."

"And then what do we do?" Ruth asked.

"I'd suppose we break the ice with him and his wife," I smiled.

For the next few minutes, Ruth and I looked more like ushers than members of the audience. We slowly walked along the aisles that surrounded the middle sections of the Eisenhower Theater. I took slow steps and took my time meticulously studying each row and each face. It was slow going, but it was the only way I could take the time to search for Representative Wilkens and his wife before the performance began. After a few minutes, I employed a strategy in my search by eliminating men with white hair in each row, since Representative Wilkens had dark hair.

It was a tedious process for two older ladies in glasses, stepping from one row to the next while trying to glimpse at each face in attendance. Another challenge was to ignore the occasional offers from well-meaning people to help me find my seat. Given how we must have looked, I could understand those kind gestures. Still it was only fourteen rows that Ruth and I had to examine, so I politely declined any help and kept my focus on the faces and the men with dark thinning hair.

After a few more minutes of searching in vain I began to doubt myself. I began to wonder if I might have been mistaken when I'd overheard the phone call and the reservations being made. Then I thought that maybe I had misjudged the character of Representative Wilkens. Perhaps he was sitting in the cheap seats with his wife after all, rather than treating her to better seats for the performance. I began to ponder that possibility when I felt my wrist being grabbed by a nice middle-aged woman in a black dress that hugged her thin frame.

"Are you lost, dear?" she asked.

It was a woman who looked to be maybe ten years younger than me. With her dark black dress and matching hair, her lips parted into a smile when I looked at her.

"Just looking for a friend," I stated with a smile.

"Does your friend have a name?" she asked.

"Yes, I'm trying to find Representative Gerald Wilkens," I replied.

The woman nodded and waved me towards the stage.

"A few rows further down and you'll find him," she directed.

I continued my search knowing full well that part of the trappings of being old and observant was to solicit help from other people. It was the appearance of confusion that tended to attract good natured assistance. I was hoping this tactic would work one more time when I found the Mrs. Wilkens.

Just as that nice lady promised, I found Representative Wilkens and his wife seated in the third row from the front. I gestured for Ruth to come over to the aisle where I was standing. When she reached me, I pointed to a few rows down from where we were standing. I could easily see the back of Representative Wilken's head, distinguished by the dark hair standing straight up on his head like tall grass in a field. He and his wife were seated at the end of the row.

"There he is," Ruth whispered. "Now what do we do?"

"Do you have our ticket stubs?" I asked.

"Of course," Ruth nodded.

"Can I have them, please," I stated.

"Why?" Ruth asked.

"Because we want to claim our seats," I replied.

"But the seats are printed right there," Ruth said, pointing to the tickets and gesturing to the other side of the aisle. "Our section is over there."

"Is it?" I grinned.

I quietly led Ruth down to the row where Representative Wilkens was seated with his wife. I stood in the aisle right beside him and waited for him to look up at us. When he turned towards me, he didn't say a word. I could tell by the expression on his face that he was both surprised and annoyed by our presence. When Mrs. Wilkens turned her head, she locked eyes with mine and offered a polite measured smile. In fact, it took his wife to elbow him before the Representative finally looked at us and said something.

"Do you ladies…need…some help?" he reluctantly asked.

"I'm so sorry," I laughed, waving my ticket stubs in the air. "I believe that the seats you're sitting in belong to us."

Mr. Wilkens turned and glared at me. The expression on his face, not to mention the size of his eyes, told me he had gone from being annoyed to downright angry. His wife's face, on the other hand, melted into the kind of warm genuine smile that her husband seemed incapable of making.

"I think you ladies might be confused," she said with a sweet voice.

"No," I answered with the sweetest expression I could muster and I waved the tickets in the air again. "We have our tickets and it appears that these *are* our seats."

"Well, my husband bought our tickets," Mrs. Wilkens replied, casting a sharp glance to her spouse. "Check them, Gerald. Are we in the right seats?"

"Of course we are," he grunted, reaching into the breast pocket of his suit and pulling out the tickets. He quietly handed them over to his wife for her to examine.

'I'm sorry, ladies," the wife replied, standing up and leaning over her husband. "According to our tickets my husband and I are in the right seats. You can check the numbers if you'd like. They're correct."

Mrs. Wilkens handed them to me and I pretended to examine them before handing them back to her.

"Well…if they are correct…can you read these numbers? My sister and I are really lost and I left my better pair of glasses at home," I said in an attempt to appeal to the sympathetic side of Mrs. Wilkens.

"Of course," she answered, and she quickly stood up, took our tickets and held them close to her face to examine. Her husband didn't move.

"My, that's a lovely necklace you're wearing," I quickly complimented.

"Thank you," Mrs. Wilkens grinned, before pointing at one of the ticket stubs. "Just looking at these numbers I think you two should find your seats over there."

She handed us our tickets and pointed to another section across the aisle from them.

"My goodness," I laughed, holding the tickets up to my eyes. "That nine on my ticket looked like a seven to me. I am so sorry. I lost my good glasses today and these replacements aren't doing the job. I apologize for my poor eyesight and the fuss I caused."

"Not a problem. I'm glad I could help you," she said with a wave of her hand. "Would you like me to walk you two ladies over and help you find your seats?"

"That won't be necessary," I smiled, knowing that in less than two minutes I had won some measure of Mrs. Wilkens's trust. I glanced at her husband, staring straight ahead, then turned back to his wife and looked her up and down. "That is a very pretty dress you have on this evening. I can't help but notice how it matches the auburn tones in your hair."

"Well, thank you," Mrs. Wilkens laughed, glancing over at her husband. "You see Gerald, this nice woman has paid me more compliments in one minute than you did all week. I just bought the dress three days ago but my husband was too busy with work to even say anything about it. I doubt he even noticed."

"I noticed," Representative Wilkens weakly said.

"Well, what he lacks as a husband he more than makes up for as a boss," I observed.

"How so?" she asked. "Do you work in my husband's office?"

"No," I answered, "but your husband does have my best friend's granddaughter working for him as an intern."

"No, I don't," he mumbled, still staring straight ahead.

"Of course you do. Her name is Megan Granger," I blurted out. "Have you ever heard that name, Mrs. Wilkens?"

My question led Representative Wilkens's jaw to lock and his eyes to narrow, but he still refused to look at us.

"No," she replied, glancing to her husband and then back to me. "So you say she's your granddaughter?"

"A friend's granddaughter," I corrected. "Megan has been an intern in your husband's office for quite some time. Isn't that right, Representative Wilkens?"

He sat silent with his gaze fixed on the stage.

"I'm afraid you have me confused with Representative Hash's office," Representative Wilkens finally spoke in a stern tone.

"I'm sorry," I laughed. "You mean Megan Granger doesn't work for you? Perhaps I did get my Representatives mixed up. There are so many of you. I guess I can't blame my glasses for that confusion."

I noticed my comment caused Mrs. Wilkens to smile, which told me that she had a good heart if she could dismiss two mistakes in three minutes.

"You don't have to apologize," she said with a wave of her hand.

"Your husband has a good memory," I observed. "Even though that girl doesn't work in his office...he still remembered her name. She certainly must have made a good impression on you, Representative Wilkens."

"I work with Representative Hash's office quite a bit," he replied, finally looking at me for the first time.

"And you can recall Megan Granger from all the other members of her staff," I smiled. "How nice of you to be so considerate of the interns."

Suddenly the lights in the theater dimmed once, indicating the show was about to begin. I quickly stepped back from Mrs. Wilkens and looked around.

"Well, it was delightful to meet you, Mrs. Wilkens," I said.

"Yes, you are a charming young lady," Ruth added.

"I'm sorry," Mrs. Wilkens said and she shook her head. "What are your names?"

"We're the Dupree sisters," I stated. "My name is Charlotte and this is my sister, Ruth. With any luck, perhaps we'll cross paths again."

I made a point of looking at Representative Wilkens after saying those words. He remained in his seat, rigid as a corpse, and just glared at me. He looked at us with the kind of expression one would normally reserve for dismissing a wayward fly. Ruth and I turned and quickly left to find our seats before the performance began.

"You said Megan's name enough," Ruth observed.

"I wanted to put a bug in Mrs. Wilkens's ear," I replied.

"I think you put a bug in his pants," Ruth giggled. "He looked rather uncomfortable."

"As well he should," I remarked.

When we found our seats, my mind was still reviewing every detail of our meeting with Representative Wilkens and his wife. I thought back on Mrs. Wilkens' every word and sentiment. Her thoughts and gestures gave me plenty to ponder when the ballet began. However, as is often the case with art, my mind soon was swept up by the performance. My heart was carried away by the story, the music and the passion that one would come to expect from a quality ballet performance.

Chapter 20:  INTERMISSION

The show that night was simply captivating. If you know me, this is not a surprising critique. Ever since I was a girl, ballets have always entranced me. The lights, the music, the way the performers move all combine to fill my heart with feelings that make me want to close my eyes and float away. That's one pleasure about attending the ballet that has not faded with the passing years. The joy I feel from watching a quality performance can still reduce me to that young girl I used to be sitting in a theater with my mouth hanging open.

On this particular evening, when intermission arrived, most people took the time to stand, stretch their legs, and socialize. A few of them walked around to meet, greet, and smile at fellow members of Washington society. Normally, I would do the same. However, on this night, I found my mind was intent on finding Representative Wilkens and his wife. While I was pleased at the thought of getting an opportunity to speak with her, I wanted to talk with him some more too. So when the intermission came, I glanced down at the row where the Wilkens were seated. I quickly noticed that they had already slipped out ahead of the rest of the audience.

"They're gone," I whispered to myself.

I quickly turned to the back of the theater that led to the main lobby in a last-ditch attempt to spot them heading out the exits. Heads were flowing out at a brisk pace in anticipation of the second act beginning in a few minutes, but I couldn't spot the Representative and his wife.

"Charlotte," I heard Ruth say while she slowly got out of her seat. "I have to use the Ladies Room. Let's go out."

My mind told me to stay put and keep searching the theater for Representative Wilkens. My mind told me that if I found him, I'd press him for some answers about those letters. Then I turned to my sister. When I looked at Ruth's face, my heart told me to be a good sister and accompany her to the Ladies Room.

Growing up with Ruth, I know all too well that her weak bladder is not something that she can attribute to old age. In fact, ever since we were young girls I remember how mother always had to take Ruth to the restroom more than once during an opera, ballet, or other performance. In fact, my mother once remarked that the only thing standing in the way of Ruth being a well-cultured woman was her bladder.

"Do you see them anywhere?" I asked as I led Ruth up the main aisle.

"Who?" Ruth shot back.

"Representative Wilkens and his wife," I stated.

"Right now I can only think about getting to the bathroom," Ruth grumbled.

"Why God blessed you with such a small bladder I'll never know," I sighed as I reluctantly led Ruth up the main aisle.

"I wouldn't say God 'blessed' me with it," Ruth complained as she bumped by a bald-headed man in a tux. "A weak bladder is more of a curse than a blessing, sister."

Choosing to stop talking about her weak bladder in public, Ruth and I filed out of the theater and into the lobby. We turned a corner and followed the crowd into the main hall of the Kennedy Center, also known as the Hall of States.

Flags from every state in the country hung from the ceiling in the Hall of States. We made our way across the red carpeting to the ladies' room. Once Ruth slipped into the ladies' room, I stood with my hands folded behind my back and waited. I strolled around the hall and admired the accent lighting from the walls on the flags. I noted how each light was aimed up to a state flag, illuminating the colors with a perfect level of low light. I also studied the designs on each flag before glancing back at the ladies' room in hopes of spotting Ruth. I waited for a few minutes watching women flow in and out of the bathroom. Then I saw one familiar face emerge from the ladies' room that caught my eye. Much to my surprise I saw Senator Wilkens' wife emerge from the bathroom.

She stood alone for a few minutes, her head turning from side to side. Her eyes danced around and I could only guess that she was searching for her husband. While she never spotted him, she did see me and, much to my surprise, smiled. I waved and smiled back. Then I realized this would be the perfect opportunity to appeal to her good nature one more time. So I approached her with a simple request.

"Have you seen my sister in there, Mrs. Wilkens?" I asked, pointing back to the bathroom.

"Your sister?" she asked.

"Yes," I nodded. "Do you remember how we thought you were sitting in our seats before the program? My sister was standing right beside me when we compared our tickets? Do you remember her, Mrs. Wilkens?"

"Oh, yes," she smiled and she put her hand on my shoulder. "Please, call me Abbie. When I hear Mrs.

Wilkins, I think my mother-in-law is lurking behind me."

"Okay…Abbie," I smiled, pointing to the bathroom. "You see, my sister, Ruth, has been in there for a very long time. Would you be kind enough to go in and call out her name a few times for me, just so I know she's alright? There are so many people in there I'm afraid I might trip over someone's foot and fall. I'm very unsteady in crowds."

"Of course I'll check," Abbie replied. "Before the show, my husband told me your last name was Dupree. So your sister is Ruth and…what's your name again?"

"Charlotte," I said, smiling at the revelation that Abbie was now taking an interest in learning my name.

"Okay, Charlotte, wait here and I'll be right back," Abbie instructed before stepping through a mob of women coming out of the restroom.

I stood and returned a few smiles to people passing by me. While I waited I was struck by the warmth and kind nature of Mrs. Wilkens. It seemed to me that Representative Wilkens was quite lucky to have found such a nice spouse. Given his philandering nature, I actually felt a twinge of sadness for her.

"We need to talk about boundaries!" I heard a man's voice snap.

I looked to my right to see Representative Wilkens standing next to me with a none too friendly look on his face. He gently took my arm and pulled me closer to him. I was close enough to see my reflection in the lenses of his glasses which appeared to be sliding down the slope of his nose.

"Are you enjoying the show?" I asked, pulling my arm from his grasp.

"No…I'm not," he replied, his eyebrow sinking lower. "You see these two meddling old women keep stalking me and my wife…so I'm a bit distracted tonight. I wanted to make this a special evening for my wife and you two are ruining it."

"What a pity," I replied, looking back at the ladies' room. "At least I know you have a conscience. Most men who run around on their wives wouldn't even try to give them a special evening out. Perhaps your guilt is catching up to you."

He unbuttoned his suit coat and tucked his hands in his pockets.

"Well...I do need her," he said in a soft voice.

For a brief second I thought he was speaking from his heart, and that he still loved his wife, which surprised me. However, my perceived surprise over this man's character lasted for about two seconds.

"You see, my district is conservative and preaches family values," Representative Wilkens continued. "If news got out that I was getting a divorce because of my affair...it would make things very difficult for me to stay in Washington."

"I agree with you on that point," I nodded and my heart began to race after hearing such a self-serving comment. "It would be hard for you to win an election."

"Are you sure I can't offer you something to leave us alone? Name your price," he said in a voice that sounded more desperate than angry.

"Money isn't an issue," I replied. "My sister and I are very comfortable, thank you. Let me make one thing perfectly clear, sir. I'm not trying to expose your affair. I simply want the names of the people who *knew* about your affair. I worked in the House and I know how word travels around those long marbled halls."

"No one knew," Representative Wilkens replied with a matter of fact tone. "We were very discreet. The only person I confided in was my chief of staff, Royce White, which I told you about before. Royce is running my re-election campaign which is why I thought it was important for him to know about my relationship with Megan."

"And what did he say?" I asked.

"Of course he was stunned," Representative Wilkens recalled. "Then he told me to stop seeing her, which I did."

"I noticed that she still has your number on her phone," I observed.

"I can't control that," he shrugged. "All I know is our relationship ended weeks ago and now I'm trying to lay the groundwork for my campaign."

"I'm sure that means getting back on your wife's good side…if she lets you," I added.

I looked at his face and I wanted to reach over and slap him. This man who came to Washington to romance a young college girl was not the least bit interested in how his indiscretions impacted others. Instead, he was only indulging in young love with his intern before discarding her to focus on his re-election campaign. Not one kind word about Megan ever left his lips. Not even one hint of remorse in how he spoke about his wife. The only sorrow he felt was over the possibility of not getting re-elected.

I turned to see Ruth and Abbie emerge from the bathroom together.

"There you are," Representative Wilkens said, walking over to his wife and taking her by the hand. "I was getting worried about you. Are you feeling okay?"

"Yes," Abbie laughed. "I was just chatting with Ruth in the ladies' room. She's been in Washington a long time, Gerald. She has lots of interesting stories to share, don't you, Ruth?"

"Only the years make me interesting," Ruth smiled. "You live in Washington as long as we have, you'll find that the people you meet and the conversations you have will make for interesting stories later in life."

"I hate to interrupt," Representative Wilkens spoke up, tapping his wrist watch. "We really need to get back before intermission is over. You know how difficult it is to find our seats when the lights go down."

"You heard my husband," Abbie said, waving Ruth and me along to walk with her, "we don't want to be late."

While it was a short stroll back into the Eisenhower Theater, it was interesting to see the dynamics in our foursome. Ruth and Abbie walked in front, smiling and having a warm discussion about the performance. Representative Wilkens and I trailed behind, both of us looking grim and silent.

Later that evening, on the cab ride home, Ruth couldn't stop talking about the very sweet nature of Abbie Wilkens.

"I've often wondered what it would be like to have a daughter," Ruth sighed. "Tonight...I felt like that question was answered. Chatting with someone like Abbie, someone who shares my sense of humor and my political views on things, it just made for a wonderful evening. Oh, Charlotte it was so nice to chat with someone like that. Do you know that she even goes to Washington Redskin football games?"

"No wonder you two hit it off," I laughed. "It started at intermission, but I was surprised when she sought you out after the performance and walked out of the theater with us."

"Her hubby didn't look too happy," Ruth giggled.

"He has his reasons for looking sour," I observed. "Abbie...she's a delight."

"So sweet," Ruth nodded and then she turned to me and the smile vanished from her face. "You know, sister, I don't think I could ever imagine her...in a rage. I just can't see her angry enough to murder someone. I don't think she'd even be capable of even uttering an angry word."

I looked out the window of the cab at the city lights flickering by.

"If we tell her what her husband's been up to I could imagine some choice words flying out of her mouth!" I replied. "She has feelings like the rest of us, Ruth. I would imagine that if she knew what her husband was up to, she'd find the right level of rage to address it."

"Do you think she's the jealous type?" Ruth asked. "I mean…I always thought this was a case of mistaken identity. Maybe she walked into the house, saw the maid holding the letter from her husband…and simply attacked her thinking it was Megan."

"I…I know it's easy to think of jealousy as a motive," I stated. "After tonight, I think we'll need to regroup on this. While you were chatting with the wife, I got a name from the husband. It seems that Royce White is not only his chief of staff but also his campaign manager. Now Wilkens is worried about keeping a lid on his affair because of the upcoming campaign. In my opinion, the man doesn't care about his marriage or his affair. All he cares about is winning his election to stay in power."

"There are any number of people in our city who worry about the same thing," Ruth pointed out.

"True," I nodded. "Maybe a few who also have dirty secrets to keep."

"More than a few," Ruth laughed and she turned and looked out the cab's window. "When we get home I think we should give Mr. White a call. I think we should invite him to our house for some tea."

"You want to invite the Great White over?" I laughed. "Oh, what to serve a political shark like him. Raw meat?"

"Tuna salad!" Ruth laughed.

"We'll talk about it," I nodded. "First thing is to call him. Now if he's running a campaign, I'd imagine he might be pretty busy to accept our invitation."

"Campaign managers are never too busy to pick up a check," Ruth grinned.

The comment caught me off guard and I turned and looked at my sister in disbelief.

"You want to donate money to support this philandering Representative's election?" I asked and I could hear my voice grow slightly louder by the end of the question. I even noticed the taxi driver glance in his mirror at us.

"A small sacrifice for the truth," Ruth replied.

We grew silent and watched the traffic lights flicker by our windows as our taxi headed to our home. In the distance, I could see the Jefferson Memorial, illuminated and milky white, looking out on the dark waters of the Potomac River. After a few seconds, Ruth elbowed me and I turned to look at her.

"Did you *really* tell Abbie Wilkens to come into the bathroom and yell my name?" she asked.

"Well...at the time it seemed like a good idea," I replied.

"Really, sister," Ruth grumbled and looked back at the window. "You could have simply talked to her until I came out. Having to answer to my name from a bathroom stall with a group of ladies standing around...even I must admit that was a bit embarrassing."

"Growing up together, I can't say that I remember anything ever embarrassing you, sister," I observed.

"Well, I guess even I have my limits," Ruth replied.

Chapter 21:  THE UNCOMFORTABLE GUEST

So there we were, quite relaxed in our favorite chairs enjoying the view from the bay window of our sitting room, waiting for our guest to arrive. It was quite unusual for us to be lounging before entertaining someone. Normally when we entertain, Ruth and I like to go through a mental checklist before welcoming someone into our home. It's a list of things that we find most helpful in putting a guest at ease.

The first item to check off involves light cleaning and tidying up. While this sounds like tedious work it really doesn't take us all that long to do. Mother taught Ruth and me the value of an organized home, which is how we live. This makes cleaning our house a little less time consuming because of our organizational habits. It also means we don't have to employ a maid.

Once completed, the next task to undertake is deciding what light refreshments to serve. Experience has taught both of us that an empty stomach and a dry mouth tend to make for less interesting conversations. So, a thorough discussion on what foods or drinks to offer usually results in a walk down to the local store or market.

The final item on our list of preparations involves identifying some interesting topics for discussion. This requires me to be sensitive to the local gossip and whether any part of that gossip would offend our guest. After all, without good conversation we're just staring at each other like cows in a field.

While Ruth and I find such a list to be quite helpful in preparing for most of our guests, we didn't really bother with cleaning or preparing food to impress this particular individual. There was no reason to make this guest feel welcome or at ease. In fact, we were thoroughly prepared to do just the opposite. Perhaps that was why we found ourselves settled in our favorite chairs, watching the clock, waiting for a knock on the door. While we waited, the clock on the mantle ticked. Mezzo curled up on the floor. Oliver hopped up on the ledge by the bay window and sat down to enjoy the view of the street. Finally, a knock from our front door brought all of us to our feet.

Ruth reached the door first and when she opened it, we found a young man with wavy blond hair and blue eyes standing on our front porch. He was dressed in a dark suit, matching overcoat with a pleasant look on his face. When I first heard the name Charles White I expected an older man, maybe balding, with a pot belly and glasses. However, the Charles White standing on our front porch looked all of twenty-one. He was trim with tan skin and a dimple at the center of his chin. He offered a courteous smile without revealing his teeth. We returned the smile with a measured expression of welcome on our faces.

"Come in," was all I could think of to say and I pushed the front door open wider.

Mr. White quickly stepped inside without saying a word.

"Call me Charlie," he said while moving past us.

"Or would you prefer Great White?" Ruth asked.

"Ahh that nickname," he said, revealing a smile of perfect white teeth. "Don't believe everything you read from the press. I won't bite."

We watched him turn and look around the hallway.

"He looks like a model," I whispered.

"He looks like a boy," Ruth whispered back.

I pressed my finger to my lips in a gesture that big sisters normally use to tell their little sisters to keep their opinions to themselves. This was especially necessary for my outspoken sister. Ruth quietly ushered our guest into the sitting room.

"Thank you for taking the time to see us," I heard her say as I entered the room behind her and Mr. White.

"It is I who should be thanking you," Mr. White replied while checking for messages on his phone. "I'm well aware of how generous both of you have been over the years when it comes to candidates that you support. I think I speak for Representative Wilkens when I say how happy he is to have your backing in his bid for re-election."

"We're happy to give it," Ruth smiled back, her eyes glancing over to me in such a way that I knew she was fibbing behind her grin.

"Please, sit down," I said, pointing to a cream-colored couch across from our favorite chairs. "My sister and I have been pleased with Representative Wilkens' voting record on issues that matter to us. However, there is one thing we are concerned about."

"And what's that?" Mr. White asked while sitting down on the couch.

"His character," I replied.

My comment caused any semblance of a smile to leave Mr. White's face while he tucked his phone into his coat pocket.

"Character?" he replied, slowly leaning forward, elbows on his knees. "When it comes to character I can assure you both that Representative Wilkens is the best candidate you will find, ladies. He loves America and has served with honor."

I could feel my head start to throb after hearing such a preprogrammed reply. I looked at my sister and she was already rubbing her forehead.

"May I interject for a moment?" I sighed and I raised my hand in the air the way a student might ask a question. "You seem like a nice young man, so let me set you straight on one rule my sister and I have in this house. Political slogans don't work in here. My sister and I were born and raised in Washington. We've met many presidents. We've met more senators and representatives than you can imagine. We're socially well connected to every rumor that floats around this town and, with that in mind, we're concerned about the things we've been hearing about your candidate. So please don't give us any more...rhetoric. It simply makes me want to reach for an aspirin. Save those lines for the county fairs and folks that live outside of D.C. Give us meaningful dialogue or you won't be getting a cent when you leave here today."

I watched Mr. White move uncomfortably in his seat, like something sharp was jabbing him in the back. He crossed one leg over the other, rubbed his chin and his eyes narrowed.

"Well, then...I'll need some specifics, ladies," he finally mumbled before settling back in the sofa.

"You want us to be blunt?" Ruth asked.

Mr. White remained silent and stared at both of us. Ruth looked at me. I knew what she was thinking and I simply nodded.

"Representative Hash has an intern," Ruth spoke in a direct tone of voice.

"My sister and I have heard some naughty things about this college intern. Her name is Megan Granger. We hear she's having an affair with Representative Wilkens," I stated, glancing over to Ruth. "Now...tell us more."

"Don't believe everything you hear!" Mr. White quickly snapped, pulling out his phone and checking it almost as an excuse to break eye contact with us.

"And why not?" I asked.

"Because it's a rumor spread by people out to ruin a good man," Mr. White sighed, putting his phone away again.

"And who would want to do that?" Ruth asked.

"An illegal alien working as a maid," Mr. White stated.

Ruth and I looked at each other. Neither one of us expected that response.

"A maid?" I asked, feeling myself lean forward the way I often do when something draws me into a conversation.

"Tell us more," Ruth said.

"It all started about a month ago. I started getting phone calls from a number I didn't recognize," Mr. White recalled. "When I finally answered, I learned that it was the maid who was employed by this...Megan Granger. I mean, her grandmother employed the maid. Anyway, what this maid told me was unsettling to hear."

"And what did she say?' Ruth asked.

"She knew about the affair between Representative Wilkens and...Miss Granger," he stated. "She told me she learned about it from a stray letter in Miss Granger's room. Then she overheard Miss Granger on her phone one evening and what she heard confirmed her suspicions. The maid went on to explain that she followed Miss Granger one evening and saw her meeting with Representative Wilkens. She took some pictures of them together. After that, the maid began calling me and then she sent me one of those pictures. When I finally confronted her about her numerous phone calls, she told me in no uncertain terms how much she wanted to keep her pictures a secret from the press. Of course, I couldn't speak of such things in front of the staff so I had to go to the Granger's home to negotiate with the maid."

"The same home that the maid was murdered in?" Ruth asked.

The comment caused the Great White to grow a bit flushed in the face.

"She was alive when I was there," he replied with the kind of commanding voice that one would typically hear in a court of law. "When I left, that maid was fine. The last time I saw her she was standing in the doorway threatening to circulate this rumor and the pictures around town until a newspaper picked it up. She told me she was friends with other maids and that maids generally held the ears of their employers when it came to rumors in Washington. I told her I'd call the police. She repeated her price. I left. You don't forget a person's face after exchanging words like that."

"Representative Wilkens tells me you were the only person who knew about his indiscretions," I stated. "Now I've met his wife and she seems very sweet. Hardly the type of person to drive a knife into someone's stomach and leave them for dead. Are you that heartless, Mr. White? I've worked in the House of Representatives. I knew many chiefs of staffs and they were very aggressive personality types. When assuming a position of power like that, it usually is not taken on by the kindest people in the room. They say you strike as quickly as a shark at your opponents. Did you smell the blood in this situation before you struck?"

"Don't let that Great White name fool you," he stated with little expression on his face. "Yes, I learned early on that it takes a tough person to lead. I also learned to be an even tougher person to say "no" to a powerful man like Representative Wilkens. I pushed him to end that relationship, ladies. I told him there was no way he would get re-elected while carrying on with a college girl. It took some convincing, but he reluctantly agreed to end the relationship. He's back with his wife and they're soon going to start seeing a marriage counselor."

"And the phone calls?" Ruth asked.

"The phone calls stopped," Mr. White continued, and a slight smile worked its way over his dimple. "I don't know why but I never try to over think a good thing when it happens. If an extortionist stops asking for money, who am I to ask why? Now I want to reassure both of you ladies, Representative Wilkens is happy to be back with his wife. He's happy to have this matter behind him and he believes he has many ideas that will make this country great again."

When he finished speaking, he looked at both of us and a wider smile re-emerged from his face in a way that I found quite unsettling. After speaking of a dead maid just a moment earlier he was still able to muster a reassuring smile.

"Very well," Ruth mumbled.

In that moment, I watched her take out her checkbook from her purse and write down a number on a check. She signed it and handed it over to Mr. White. His eyebrows dropped down. The smile vanished as quickly as it came. He looked at Ruth the way a small child does when a curious thing happens.

"What is this? A joke?" he asked, nervously brushing his hand through his thick blond hair.

"Good faith money," Ruth replied, pointing to the check. "We will need to ask some questions of our own before we can fully support Representative Wilkens. It would help us feel more...comfortable with our decision."

"But...twenty-five dollars?" he laughed, waving the check in the air.

"Like my sister said...more to come," I smiled, standing up and gesturing for our guest to stand and follow us into the hallway. "Of course, despite what you've told us, my sister and I are still concerned about the character issue. We simply want to ask more questions, Mr. White."

"I...I understand," he said, standing up. He moved into the hallway and hesitated, unsure of which way to turn for the front door.

"Do you know what Franklin Roosevelt once said about investing in real estate?" Ruth asked, pointing him in the right direction.

"I can't imagine," Mr. White mumbled as he stepped towards the door.

"He said it can be, 'Purchased with common sense, paid for in full, and managed with reasonable care.' He also called it 'the safest investment in the world,' if I remember correctly," Ruth explained.

"That's what we want for our money, Mr. White," I explained. "We want a safe investment that has been made with common sense. When we convince ourselves that this is the case with Representative Wilkens, we will contact you with a more...substantial investment."

With those final words, I opened the door and watched Mr. White leave without so much as a thought to express.

"The Great White looked perturbed," Ruth giggled. "Like he could chew on some raw meat."

"He's under pressure," I replied while closing the door. "He's running a re-election campaign. Time is important to him. I can understand his frustration with us. I can also understand his rationale for wanting the maid dead. He has a motive. Now we need to prove if he did it."

"How?" Ruth asked.

"I...I guess we'll need to attend some social events and ask some question about our new friend, Mr. White. We'll see if anyone of our friends can speak about his temperament and whether he would be the kind of person to step over the line.

Chapter 22: LUNCH WITH MALCOLM

Malcolm Watson was like any other man who was about to retire from his job. He served with great distinction at his place of employment. He was well liked by co-workers and colleagues. He'd earned the respect of other professionals in his field. And now, after many years, Malcolm Watson was going to retire. Oh, and as if I need to mention it, he was also a respected member of the United States Supreme Court.

As lifelong residents of Washington, Ruth and I had met Justice Watson on more than one occasion. When we've spoken, I've always found him and his wife, Sunny, to be very friendly and good conversationalists. When he announced his intent to retire, the newspapers were packed with facts about Justice Watson and his life. From the articles I read, combined with my own experiences in meeting him, I always thought Justice Watson was a good man.

While being a Supreme Court Justice can be a lifetime appointment, I admired Justice Watson's perspective in seeing the bigger picture. Every article I read indicated to me that Justice Watson knew there was a world beyond our shores and he wanted to experience it. There were family members he wanted to spend more time with, too.

There were also hobbies and interests he wanted to connect with again. He was also frequently quoted about wanting to spend more time with his wife. From everything I read, and from what I'd heard from friends, Justice Watson's reasons for retirement were grounded in a good heart.

So when Ruth and I received a phone call from a friend inviting us to a luncheon to celebrate Justice Watson's years of service, we were thrilled to accept. Any opportunity to see the Watsons was always a pleasure for me and my sister. I personally saw it as an opportunity to focus on something other than the Megan Granger situation.

A few days later, Ruth and I found ourselves seated at a long table with a few of Justice Watson's closest friends. We dined in *The Monocle Restaurant*, a fine establishment that has been in Washington for more than fifty years. It was a place that, when it first opened, had two new young Congressmen who enjoyed the food and came on a regular basis. Their names were Richard Nixon and John Kennedy.

For this particular event, I was seated next to Ruth and a rather large gentleman who quickly introduced himself as Hank from Maine. No last name, just Hank from Maine. In addition to not telling me his last name, Hank from Maine also failed to explain his connection to Justice Watson. It was a curiosity I chose not to pursue once the waitress arrived. Hank didn't hesitate to order a steak and potatoes for dinner. The fact that he didn't hesitate, left me to quickly review the menu before ordering the Shellfish Bisque and a side salad.

During the interim between ordering and waiting for our food, Justice Watson came around to each guest, thanking everyone for coming and advising us to enjoy the evening since he was paying. When he spoke to Ruth and me, he recalled the many years we'd associated with him. How, it seemed to him, the three of us grew up and grew old in this town together. He concluded by thanking us for being two constant sources of friendship in a town that is always changing.

Eventually our food arrived. While my soup smelled delicious, I couldn't take my eyes off of Hank's meal. His steak was huge and the baked potato accompanying it was also rather large. I sat there mentally counting how many calories this man was about to eat, before grinning at my more modest order of soup and salad.

"I hope he likes going back to those New England winters," I heard Hank laugh before snapping a rather large piece of steak from his fork. "Malcolm says he wants to go back to Maine to live, but it's been a long time since he felt a New England winter. Most retirees move south, don't they?"

"That huge mansion that he and Sunny bought...they won't even have to step outside until spring," observed another man from across the table and he chuckled at his own words.

"Winter is winter," I observed as I undid my napkin and fixed it on my lap. "I can't imagine much of a difference between a snowstorm here and one in Maine."

"That's cuz you're not from Maine," Hank laughed while chomping down another piece of steak. "You're all skin and bones, ma'am. You wouldn't last a week up there when a storm comes pouring off the Atlantic or when the winds come racing down from Canada."

I looked at Hank, who was now chewing steak with the vigor of a horse, and simply smiled at him.

"I'll take your word for it. I've never been to New England in the winter." I nodded before scooping up some of my soup.

"You're a smart one," he said with a wink in my direction while still chewing.

I turned to my left where Ruth was eating a salad and listening intently to two ladies talking about Justice Watson as a husband. I then craned my neck down to the far end of the table where Justice Watson was seated. As far as I could tell, Ruth and I were the only faces from Washington in the room.

*Why did he invite us?* I asked myself.

Ruth quickly turned and looked at me.

"You know he's always enjoyed my sense of humor," Ruth stated and she shrugged her shoulders once.

"Oh really?" I asked, feeling my eyebrows go up.

"Sure he does," Ruth mumbled. "Besides, the faces in this town change with every election the way the leaves change every season. We've been constants for him in the decades he's served. That's why he invited us."

"I suppose you're right," I nodded, before sipping more of my soup.

"He will be missed," Ruth sighed.

"I think it's wonderful what he's doing," one woman observed. "Retiring to spend more time with his family. Especially his wife."

"He's a good man," Ruth replied.

"Yes," the other woman nodded. "We've known Malcom and Sunny long before they came to Washington. Sunny has supported him for many years. She loves him more than anything. You know how it is when you're in love. I can't begin to tell you all of the sacrifices Sunny has made for Malcom's legal career."

The woman paused for a second, leaned forward and glared at Hank.

"Hank!" she called out. "Stop eating and tell this nice lady what I mean."

Hank hesitated with a fork full of steak long enough to grunt, "Yes, Sunny has always supported Malcolm. She's a good wife."

With those few words, another chunk of steak vanished into Hank's mouth.

"Forgive my husband's manners," the woman sighed, glaring at Hank. "I know a lot of feminists might have a problem with a wife giving up her career to support her husband, but I don't have a problem with it. It's quite simple really. When you love someone you'll do anything for them. Do you see anything wrong with that, Mrs. Dupree?"

"It's Miss Dupree," I corrected. "And…no…I can't image what it would be like to love someone so deeply that you'd do *anything* for them."

After hearing what Hank's wife had to say about the things we do for the people we love, I saw the face of Megan Granger emerge in my mind and linger in my thoughts. She was a young woman who loved someone. What sacrifices had she made out of her love for Representative Wilkens? What kind of actions would she still take out of her love for him? It was a question I couldn't shake for the rest of the evening.

Chapter 23: SLEEPLESS AT MIDNIGHT

That night, after our dinner with Malcom, I had trouble falling asleep. When a thought keeps me up at night, it's a nagging problem to shake. After tossing and turning with my eyes closed, it simply became a futile effort. Thoughts about Megan kept swirling in my head. Thoughts that were simply too interesting to ignore. Finally, I got out of bed, and tried to find something around the house to help my mind slow down.

I eventually found my way into the kitchen, where I made myself some warm milk and grabbed two cookies from the cookie jar. I sat down at the kitchen table and took in the silence. It was half past midnight and I was sipping some warm milk and nibbling on an oatmeal cookies like I did as a school girl. I was not the only one who couldn't sleep. Mezzo strolled into the kitchen, her fluffy tail dangling from side to side while she walked. She hopped up on the kitchen table, sat down and looked at me eye to eye.

"You can't sleep either?" I asked Mezzo.

The cat simply stared at me while I took a small bite of my cookie.

"You've been a good cat with our houseguest," I explained in between bites. "In fact, I must say that you've been more than patient."

Mezzo stared at me, her tail brushing across the table top.

"I'm quite certain you'd like your life to go back to normal," I said before taking a sip of warm milk while gently petting Mezzo's head. "I don't know why Oliver doesn't like you. I like you. You're a good cat. I wish I could make Oliver see that…but I can't."

Again, Mezzo sat and stared at me, her eyes growing heavy. Watching Mezzo grow sleepy brought out a yawn from my lips.

I couldn't help but ponder both situations. Whether it was getting Oliver to not fight with Mezzo, or getting Megan Granger to meet with us without her grandmother, they were both challenges that needed to be resolved.

"You know," I told Mezzo after taking another sip of milk, "it seems to me that free will is the challenge in both of our situations. How do we get Oliver to like you? How do we *make* Oliver like you? How do we get Megan to meet with us? How do we *make* her want to meet with us?"

I took another nibble of my cookie and pondered those questions. I took another sip of milk and my eyes turned from Mezzo sitting on the kitchen table beside me to the center of the table where I saw the small stack of mail collected from Lana's home. I reached out and grabbed hold of one of those naughty letters and looked it over.

"Disgusting," I said to Mezzo before jamming the letter into the envelope.

I slid the envelope back across the table to where the pile of letters sat. I sat and stared at the envelopes and the words printed on them. Then, a thought popped into my head. A thought that made me reach over and grab all the envelopes that contained those naughty letters. I spread the envelopes out on the table and let my eyes move from one letter to the next. I looked at the name and address on each envelope. I noted the curve in the way the letters were written. I also noticed how the numbers on the envelope were written. Soon I had a plan for what to do about Megan.

Chapter 24:  TWO DAYS LATER

Kogod Courtyard is a little-known gem to those who live outside the beltway. Funded by Washington philanthropists Robert and Arlene Kogod, it is an enclosed courtyard that, in our opinion, is a wonder of engineering. For Ruth and me, it's like stepping into an oasis.

Nestled between the Smithsonian American Art Museum and the National Portrait Gallery, the Kogod Courtyard is 28,000 square feet of springtime captured in a temperature-controlled setting for people to visit year round. In addition to the mild temperature, visitors also get to savor the natural sunlight that slips through a magnificent wavy glass ceiling. The unusual shape of the ceiling also acts as an absorbent to keep the reverberation level at a minimum. Because of the climate controls and the sunshine, trees and shrubs are maintained year-round for visitors to enjoy. Tables and chairs are scattered around the courtyard for people to sit and enjoy the setting. People can even savor good food served from a café in the courtyard. During the dark days of winter Ruth and I find that visiting the National Gallery, followed by lunch in Kogod Courtyard, makes for a most satisfying day. In our opinion, there is nothing more pleasurable to do in the winter.

Having been to Kogod Courtyard many times, Ruth and I are quite familiar with the types of people who frequent it. Since it is a calming place, we've noticed few if any politicians or political insiders. Living in

Washington as long as we have, Ruth and I know all the faces when we spot them. It seems to me that the courtyard is simply too calming a place for political insiders. Yet, we do notice that Kogod Courtyard attracts a different set of Washington residents.

We see lots of young families who bring small children to run and play in the courtyard. We also see art aficionados who wander aimlessly through this area after visiting one of the Smithsonian galleries. On occasion, I've even seen a few people who carry a book or a newspaper to read while they enjoy the silence of this facility.

A feature I like is how the shape of the roof lends to absorbing sounds. A child's squeal is simply not as loud. It always sounds like people are speaking in hushed tones. There are no echoes from one end of the courtyard to the other. Taking all of this into consideration, I thought it would be the perfect place to meet with Megan Granger.

Of course, we simply couldn't call her on the phone and invite her to join us. We needed a more creative inducement to get her to the Kogod Courtyard. Thanks to my late night with Mezzo, I believed I'd found that inducement.

Ruth and I took a seat at one table and grinned at the young children playing around us. We talked about how, no matter what time of the year we went, the spacious surroundings of Kogod Courtyard always seemed to invigorate children to run, yell and play. In between enjoying their laughter and squeals, I'd check my watch. Finally, after checking my watch for the fourth or fifth time I looked across the table at Ruth and smiled.

"It's five minutes to three," I stated.

"And?" Ruth asked.

"She should be here soon," I casually replied.

"Aren't you confident?" Ruth laughed.

I quietly nodded while my eyes scanned the scene. Specifically, I was looking at both entrances to the courtyard from the surrounding buildings. I scanned the scenery for any sign of Megan Granger.

"You really think she's going to be here?" Ruth asked with a hint of skepticism in her words. "With everything that's happened she'd be taking a big risk by doing it."

"I think she'll be here," I sighed, keeping my eyes on the entrances. "Like someone told me at Malcolm Watson's luncheon, people under the spell of romance will do anything for the person they love."

About thirty seconds after speaking those words, I saw Megan finally enter the courtyard. She was easy to spot in her high heels, a navy blue dress that went down to her knees and a white scarf hanging loosely around her neck. What distinguished her from the crowd was how quickly she was walking around. The calming atmosphere of Kogod Courtyard could not work its magic on Megan. She walked quite fast, sidestepping one wayward child while maintaining her brisk pace. Unlike the other people in the courtyard, she was not here to relax or admire the surroundings. Ruth and I watched Megan walk up one end of the courtyard and back again, her head whipping from side to side. When she made eye contact with us, she stopped in her tracks for the first time and just stared.

"Let's invite her over," Ruth suggested.

Ruth stood up and waved Megan over to our table. Despite our gestures, Megan remained in the middle of the courtyard, her head turning from side to side. Then she slowly took a few uncertain steps in our direction while she continued to study the faces that circulated around her. When she reached our table, she looked at us but didn't smile. I'd describe her demeanor as a polite expression of confusion.

"Good afternoon, Megan," Ruth said.

"Ladies…what a surprise to see you here," Megan stammered, her voice sounding not as confident as it had been when we toured the House with her just a few days earlier.

She made brief eye contact with us before allowing her attention to be drawn to someone walking by our table.

"Please sit down," I said, pointing to an empty chair.

"Yes, join us," Ruth chimed in.

"I can't…I'm looking for someone," Megan replied.

"No, you're not," I stated and I slid the empty chair towards her.

"What?" Megan asked, still glancing around.

"I said there's no one here for you to see," I explained.

Megan continued to not make eye contact with me and was only half listening to my words. Finally I stood up and stepped in front of her face.

"Look at me, Megan," I finally said. When her blue eyes did just that I shook my head. "Representative Wilkens isn't coming here. I wrote the letter you received. I was the one who invited you, not Gerald. Now please sit down."

Megan shook her head like I'd just awakened her from a nap. She looked at me and her eyes narrowed as she tried to process this painful truth. She pulled her phone out of her purse and checked it. Her thumbs pressed at the screen and then she stopped and waited. She slowly put her phone down and glared across the table at me.

"You?" she mumbled and her head tilted to one side. "What have you done?"

"We needed to speak with you alone," I explained as I settled back down in my seat. "I had to find a way to get you here. So...I wrote you that letter."

"But...how did you make your handwriting look like Gerald's?" she asked.

"When I worked with your mother in the House," I explained, "one of my jobs was sorting mail. I did it so often I began to notice different patterns in people's handwriting. I eventually taught myself how to mimic a person's style of writing by looking at just a few words. Apparently, I'm still pretty good at it because...here you are."

The expression on Megan's face changed from curious to genuine anger. We were now beyond the point of smiling and being polite to each other. In this particular situation, she was angry and didn't mind wearing that anger in her face for me to see.

"We have questions," Ruth spoke up.

The conversation was briefly interrupted by a small child who ran by our table screaming, with his young mother chasing after him. Ruth smiled at the scene but my eyes remained locked on Megan.

"Questions about what?" Megan asked.

"Gerald," I softly stated.

She glanced down at the floor after she heard me say his name. The name of the man she had latched her heart onto.

"I...I can't talk about him," she replied and she pushed her chair back and stood up.

"We think he killed your grandmother's maid," Ruth quickly stated.

My sister's impulsive choice of words caused Megan to remain standing by our table.

"A friend of ours works for a local newspaper," Ruth continued. "We're prepared to tell him about the blackmailing that was going on between the maid and

Wilkens' office. How your boss found out and let his emotions get the better of himself. We're pretty sure he killed her to get re-elected. As we will tell the reporter, Representative Wilkens is a desperate man who will do anything for power…even murder."

"Yes," I chimed in. "The worst sort of politician. No regard for people. He's a man who just wants the power and the money and will stop at nothing to get it."

"He's not like that," Megan whimpered.

"Don't worry, Megan," I replied. "You can stop covering up for him. He can't do anything to you. One well-placed article with the right reports and the only job Representative Wilkins will find in this town is pushing a broom through the U.S. Capitol. I promise you that much!"

"What a louse!" Ruth said.

"Stop it!" Megan snapped and she looked at both of us before taking a deep breath. She sat back down again and shook her head. "You don't understand. He's not like that. You can't say those things about Gerald. He's a good man. You'll ruin him with those lies."

"Are they lies?" I asked.

"What you're accusing him of…it isn't true," Megan said, her voice quivering with each word.

"Then what is the truth?" Ruth pressed.

Megan looked up at that magnificent glass ceiling stretched over us. Her face was bright red. I could also see her eyes blinking quickly and I could tell she was on the verge of breaking down into tears. Her bottom lip began to quiver.

"Unless you can tell us something different, I'm afraid we're going to tell our friend in the press what we know and what we think happened," I explained.

"You know, Megan," Ruth chimed in, "once that story comes to light I'm sure there will be a police investigation. With an election season almost here, stories like that tend to get picked up by news sources from around the country. Everyone in America will know about you having an affair with the U.S. Representative who committed a murder. That salacious stuff will be in every tabloid!"

Megan began to cry. Her head dipped down and she covered her face with her hands and began to sob. Ruth and I glanced around to see if anyone noticed how upset Megan had become. The children continued to run and play. The mothers continued to talk. After about a minute, Megan finally looked up at us and wiped her eyes.

"You still love him?" I observed, reaching across the table and handing her a tissue.

Megan simply nodded her head and took the tissue.

"That's why I...I can't let that happen to Gerald," she sighed while wiping her nose.

"What do you mean?" I asked. "He created this problem."

"He's drunk on power," Ruth stated and she casually waved one hand in the air. "Don't feel sorry for him!"

"I can't let Gerald be blamed for what happened," Megan spoke with a hushed voice. She wiped some tears off her cheeks with both hands, sniffed once, then nodded and seemed more composed.

"Megan," I said, leaning in a little closer to her and sensing that she had something to offer. "Like my sister said, don't feel badly for him. Representative Wilkens simply stepped over the line by killing that girl. He'll be punished for it."

"You don't understand," Megan said, and she slowly leaned across the table like she was about to share a secret.

"Then help us to understand," Ruth spoke up.

"You know my grandmother was out of town," Megan began, wiping her eyes. "I had the house to myself…but I was working lots of crazy hours. Grandma made only one request of me. You see, the maid was new and grandma didn't trust giving her a key. So she asked me to let the maid in to do afternoon cleaning."

And did you?" Ruth asked.

Megan nodded.

"I ran home mid-afternoon," Megan began. "I left the front door open and went up to change into something more comfortable because I knew it was going to be a late night at the office. After I changed I laid down on the bed and I must have drifted off for a few minutes. When I woke up I heard a man's voice downstairs. It was the angry tone in his voice that woke me. It almost sounded like an argument. I got out of bed and stood at the top of the steps to listen to what was being said. When I heard them use my name and Gerald's name I was shocked. Then I heard Maria's voice. I heard her make a threat."

"Who was she talking to?" Ruth asked.

"Charles White," Megan said, and she nodded after saying his name.

"Did you go down and talk to Mr. White?" I asked.

"No," Megan replied and she sat back in her chair and her eyes glanced over at a tree not far from where we were seated. "It was clear to me what was happening from the way the conversation was going. I realized that Maria was blackmailing Gerald. When she wouldn't listen to what Mr. White said…I knew I had to confront her."

"And did you?" Ruth asked.

Megan grew silent and she folded her arms.

"I thought about it," she finally replied. "I'm pretty soft spoken. With my blond hair, blues eyes and soft voice…I know I'm not someone who tends to be taken seriously. So I knew I had to do something to get

Maria's attention. You see, Maria was just a year older than me, but she tended to treat me like her little sister. She always respected my grandmother...but never respected me."

"Respect is important," Ruth nodded. "It's our experience that in this town it really is hard for a young woman to earn respect."

"You must have been angry with what you heard," I observed.

Megan stared down at the floor and I thought she looked lost in a swell of memories. Her eyes then drifted to the side.

"I waited until Mr. White left," Megan began. "Then I walked down the steps. I could tell by the way she looked at me that Maria didn't know I was up there. She just stared at me as I came down the last step. When I walked over to her, she didn't say anything. She simply turned, grabbed a sponge and began to clean the kitchen sink."

"And then what did you do while she cleaned?" I asked.

"I...I...told her what she was doing was wrong," Megan began. "I told her Gerald was a good man and she shouldn't blackmail him. I was very angry. She didn't say anything so I told her it was none of her business. Finally, she told me she hoped Gerald was a good man which was why she thought he would pay her money to keep our relationship a secret."

I could see Megan's young face begin to grow flush and her eyes began to blink faster.

"Like I said," Megan mumbled, "just one year difference between Maria and me...but she always acted better than me. When I begged her to stop blackmailing Gerald she simply smiled and went about scrubbing that sink. When she ran out of spray I watched her reach under the sink for another canister.

That's when I decided to do something to make sure she understood how much I wanted her to leave Gerald alone. I wanted her to stop smiling, look me in the eye and be afraid."

"So what did you do?" Ruth asked.

"There was a knife block on the counter. I reached over and grabbed the longest sharpest knife I could find," Megan recalled, wiping her eyes with the back of her hand. "She finally stopped and looked at me when I held that knife between us. I told her again that I wanted her to leave Gerald alone. She smirked at me and grabbed for the knife, but I stepped back so she couldn't reach it. I wasn't sure what I was going to do. She stepped closer to me and grabbed at it. Again I stepped back. Now I could feel my back against the kitchen counter near the sink. I stared at her and she said something in Spanish, but I wasn't quite sure what she meant. And then…it happened."

"What happened?" I asked.

"Something jumped over my shoulder," Megan recalled. "Out of the corner of my eye I saw something move through the kitchen window behind the sink. It was that cat you brought around to show my grandmother. It leaped at me, clawed my shoulder and caused me to look away from Maria. At that moment, when I was looking at that cat, Maria lunged at me. I was so focused on the cat, I wasn't aware of Maria. I just…reacted. I spun away from that cat. I felt something tug at my arm. Then I saw Maria stagger back and the knife…the knife was in her stomach."

Megan put her elbows on the table between us and burst into tears. I reached across the table and put my hand on her back.

"And then," she sniffed, wiping her eyes with the tissue, "she took a few steps into the living room and dropped on the hardwood floor. The way she fell, the knife drove deeper into her stomach."

Megan rubbed her arms with her hands, as if a chill had shot through the courtyard.

"I stood there...waiting for her to take one more breath. When she didn't, all I could think about was how safe Gerald was going to be now that she was dead. So I stood there and thought about what to do. I knew I had to get the knife out. Turning her body and pulling out that knife...it was the hardest thing I ever did in my life. I pulled it out and cried the whole time. I wrapped it up in a towel and stuck it in a chest in my grandmother's attic and then went back to work."

"You went to work?" Ruth asked.

"After all that...how were you possibly able to face people in the office?" I asked, amazed that Megan was tough enough to do this.

"I went to a committee meeting that Gerald was in," Megan replied. "It was a meeting with lots of people gathered in this big room. I just sat in a corner by myself, staring at the walls, thinking about what had happened. Every few minutes, I started to cry but no one noticed. No one cared. I stayed in that meeting and took some notes for the rest of the day...and then I thought about what to do with Maria's body. I slept at the office that night. The next day when I came home I thought it was a miracle that the body was gone and the floor had been cleaned. I guess I was lucky that you two ladies came along."

"You can thank the cat for that," I replied.

"And the people your grandmother called to clean up that mess," Ruth added. "You're quite fortunate she was away for the weekend."

"Your grandmother told us you were also away for the weekend," Ruth pointed out.

"That's what I told her," Megan sniffed. "You know…she's my grandmother and I didn't want to upset her. I told Mr. White about what happened so he vouched for me working with him all weekend. I guess he didn't feel too sorry for Maria since she was blackmailing Gerald."

I looked at Ruth and she looked at me. There was one more question I had to ask.

"And…why are you telling us everything, Megan?" I asked.

"I just can't keep this to myself anymore," Megan cried and she covered those lovely blue eyes with her hands again. "I haven't slept in weeks. I'm exhausted. Every time I try to sleep all I see is Maria and all that blood."

Ruth and I sat down and let Megan continue to speak. We let her unburden everything she'd been carrying. We let her cry. We watched more children run around, completely oblivious to Megan's tears. We looked up at the last strands of sunlight slipping through the glass ceiling.

While Ruth offered some words to Megan, I looked around and took in the sense of illusion that the Kogod Courtyard provides. The comfortable temperatures and the low humidity that is maintained year round. The green leaves on the trees and the green shrubbery that is carefully maintained. The little details that helped to create the illusion of spring time all year long. Then I thought about how most illusions require many details to be believed. Then I thought about the many details that Ruth and I had uncovered to dispel the illusion of a robbery gone bad to learn the truth about the death of Maria Nunez.

## Chapter 25: LUNCH WITH LANA

A week later, Ruth and I attended a luncheon at the Hay-Adams Hotel which is located across the street from our church. As you may know, the hotel is named after Jon Hay and Henry Adams, both of whom owned houses in the very spot where the hotel was built in 1928. Little do people know that Henry Adams, in fact, was also the grandson of President John Quincy Adams.

Over the years, the Hay-Adams Hotel has established a fine reputation with those who travel in Washington's social circles. So much so that President Obama and his family chose to stay there before his first inauguration. Perhaps it was due to this fine reputation that the new First Lady decided to choose this location for such an important event.

In attending the luncheon, I was not surprised to learn that Lana Granger would also be there. Like a moth to the flame, she was never all that far away from the new First Lady's social engagements. For this occasion, the buzz around the city was that the First Lady wanted to start a campaign to champion the power of art in schools. So when Ruth and I stepped into the Hay-Adams Room where the luncheon was taking place, we were pleasantly surprised to find a wide range of children's paintings on display.

Ruth and I walked around, commenting on the quality of some of the artwork and smiling at some other efforts. We reflected on how all of the paintings were done by children of varying ages. All in all, it was the kind of exhibit that left a smile on our faces. After we took in the displays around the room, it occurred to us that most every state was represented by a framed work of art from a child.

The moment we were finished looking at the collection, Ruth decided to walk around and make light chitchat with a few familiar faces we knew from Washington society. I was not so inclined. Light chitchat and laughter really didn't interest me on this particular day. I had other things on my mind.

With Ruth gone, I wandered around the room and found my name at a large round table with other names I recognized. I placed my purse on the bright white tablecloth, sniffed the beautiful arrangement of red roses at the center of the table then sat down. I enjoyed the sweet aroma while I scanned the room for one face. After a few minutes, I spotted who I had been looking for.

Without hesitation, I stood up and made my way across the spacious room in pursuit of Lana Granger. As I suspected, I watched Lana trailing behind the First Lady in hopes of talking to her. I knew I had to get to Lana before that happened. When I got close enough, I grabbed Lana by the arm before she could make eye contact with the First Lady.

"Hey!" I heard her snap, glancing down at my hand.

"We need to talk," I replied, keeping a firm grip on her wrist. "Come with me!"

Lana managed to pull her arm away.

"You don't need to take me into a quiet corner to talk!" she snapped, folding her arms and glaring at me.

"What I have to say should be said in private," I replied and I turned and waved with one hand for her to follow me.

As I started to walk out of the ballroom I could sense her resistance lessen by the look on her face. I turned and noticed that, slowly, she was beginning to follow me. I led Lana into the nearest ladies' room. When I entered the room, I quickly checked all the stalls to see if they were empty. When Lana entered a few seconds later, I pulled the door to the ladies' room shut and locked it. Lana turned to face a mirror, pulled some lipstick from her purse and began to re-apply it. She ran her hand over her meticulously styled hair and smiled.

"Rather dramatic of you," she sighed. "Someone is going to be knocking on that door so make it quick, Sweet Dupree. You needn't lock it."

"I hate that name," I mumbled. "I've always hated that name."

Lana kept her focus on the mirror while she adjusted her hair.

"What do you want, Sweet Dupree?" Lana sighed.

"We need to talk about Megan," I began, stepping next to her. "How is she doing?"

"As you know...she has her problems," Lana said, her eyes glancing away from the mirror and towards me. "She'll land on her feet, though. After all, this is Washington...and she's a Granger. So good of you to call the police on her, Charlotte. That was a surprise to see two officers handcuff my granddaughter."

I took one step closer to Lana.

"She killed someone," I stated. "Did you know?"

"Did I know what?" Lana asked, turning back to the mirror before adjusting her necklace.

"That your granddaughter was the one who killed Maria Nunez?" I asked.

Lana sighed. She glanced down at a diamond bracelet on her slender wrist and nervously adjusted it while looking in the mirror.

"It was the weekend and I'd gone away to visit my sister in Boston," Lana sighed. "Megan told me she went out with Charles White for a weekend at his cabin.

She told the police the same thing. Mr. White vouched for her and that was that. He's quite handsome, don't you think?"

"Handsome…and as guilty as her," I observed. "So what has she told the police since then? Did she finally meet with the police to confess to killing Maria?"

Lana simply stared at me and remained silent. Slowly she turned and rechecked the stalls of the ladies' room before walking up to me. She stepped much closer than I could imagine and my eyes were drawn to how perfectly she'd applied her makeup.

"I haven't contacted the police," Lana replied with no expression on her face.

I stood toe to toe with Lana and leaned close to her ear.

"She took a life," I whispered.

"She had a fling with a married man," Lana countered.

"Your maid is dead," I pointed out.

"Yes," Lana nodded and she turned back to the mirror. "And do you know why she died, Charlotte? She died because Megan cared too much. She let her heart get in the way and she fell in love and love….doesn't let you think straight. I believe you made that mistake, once, didn't you Sweet Dupree? Isn't that why you quit working in the House? Didn't you fall in love with your boss? The only true love you probably ever had…since you never married."

The words caused me to simply shake in anger. My heart was racing and I wanted to slap Lana's smug expression right off her face. I couldn't believe she was using a murder as an opportunity to dig up something from my past to throw in my face.

"I guess I didn't train Megan well enough," Lana mumbled and she stepped over to the deadbolt on the door and unlocked it.

I stood silent while Lana walked up to the sink before washing her hands.

"You know," she began. "I hope the steak they're serving today won't be too tough. I like mine bloody and tender. How about you, Sweet Dupree?"

I stepped over to where Lana stood and pointed at the sink.

"I think you'd better keep washing your hands," I advised, pointing towards the sink.

"I'm afraid you simply can't see all the stains on them."

And with those words, I left the Golden Girl. I left her standing by the sink, smiling into the mirror at my suggestion. It's the last time I ever spoke to Lana Granger. As far as I'm concerned, it will be the last time I'll ever speak to her.

## Chapter 26:  CLOSURE AND THE CAT

When the flood of memories stopped filling her head, Charlotte took a sip of tea to sooth her sore throat and looked at her guest, who she could tell was still processing the truth about Megan Granger.

"Well," Lillian sighed before checking her watch, "that was quite a story, Charlotte. I would never have imagined something like that happening to such a young girl. You two were very lucky to uncover all of this, weren't you?"

"Well," Ruth began, "do you know what James Garfield once said about luck?"

"No," Lillian answered.

"President Garfield once said that 'a pound of pluck is worth a ton of luck.' I think Charlotte and I showed more pluck than luck in this matter. Once we started, we were determined to get to the truth."

"Agreed," Charlotte nodded.

"So whatever became of poor Megan Granger?" Lillian asked.

"As I said, we called the police and they arrested her," Charlotte nodded. "We lost track after that out of respect for the family. I must give it to Lana, though. She kept all of this out of the newspapers. I'd imagine she must have called in every favor and made every threat imaginable to give her granddaughter some privacy."

"Poor Megan," Lillian sighed.

"Yes," Charlotte nodded, "such a shame. Poor Megan allowed the lust in her heart to turn into love.

She broke the first rule for having an affair in Washington. Maria Nunez just didn't know she was playing with fire when she began to blackmail Representative Wilkens. She simply didn't know how much passion Megan was carrying in her heart for the man she loved."

"Passion is a curse of youth," Ruth chimed in.

Again, Lillian checked her watch and then scanned the room.

"While this has been fascinating…I really must get going," Lillian said, stepping away from the sisters and moving towards one end of the sitting room. "I arrived here in the morning and it's already late afternoon. My, where does the time go?"

Charlotte and Ruth watched Lillian bend down and scoop up Oliver from where he was sleeping on the floor. The cat remained calm, looking around with its paws dangling loose from Lillian's hand. She turned and opened the door to a small cage that was on the floor next to her chair. Once she placed Oliver inside the cage and closed the door, it was easy to hear Oliver's objections to his new smaller quarters. He began to meow soon after being placed in the cage. As Lillian collected her purse Oliver began to grow more vocal about his imprisonment.

"Thank you for a most enjoyable morning and afternoon," Lillian grinned, standing up with the small cage in her one hand. "And again thank you for supporting the shelter. Simply raising awareness of how we care for strays in this city will go a long way in raising funds."

"It was our pleasure," Ruth smiled.

Gesturing down the hallway, Ruth led Lillian to the front door. While they chatted some more, Charlotte trailed behind them. She kept watching Lillian carry the small cage in her one hand. Charlotte also tried to ignore Oliver's meows.

"I hope I didn't put you to sleep with my story," Charlotte apologized, trying to ignore the cat and keep her focus on her departing guest. "When I tell a story, and Ruth knows this all too well, I feel that every detail is important."

"It was worth the time to hear. I have many friends who are always interested in hearing a juicy tale about another love gone afoul in Washington," Lillian grinned.

Charlotte nodded, but her concentration was broken again by the sound of Oliver meowing. Her eyes dropped down to the cage. There she could see Oliver, his small face nestled against the front of the cage. His green eyes stared at Charlotte and she found it hard to look away. While Lillian offered her thanks one more time, and Charlotte nodded at all the right times, her mind remained focused on the cat.

Following Lillian out to the front porch, Charlotte saw Oliver's gray face peer out from behind the narrow bars of the carrying case. His green eyes looked around the porch, as if taking in each detail, perhaps sensing he was about to leave. Then Oliver stopped meowing. He turned his eyes to Charlotte one more time. In that moment, Charlotte felt something in her heart tug at her better nature. A warm feeling that sent a smile across her face.

"Good day, Dupree sisters," Lillian said before descending down the steps from the front porch. Charlotte watched her guest head towards the front gate with the heavy carry cage that caused her to walk awkwardly.

"Wait!" Charlotte finally called out, stepping off the front porch with Ruth behind, following behind her.

"Yes?" Lillian said by the gate.

Charlotte clenched her hands in front of her waist and took one small measured step closer to Lillian. She took a deep breath and mustered up the courage to say the words that had been lingering in her head.

"I think…Oliver should stay with us," Charlotte softly said, looking down at the carrying case in Lillian's hand.

"What?" Ruth asked and her head quickly snapped in Charlotte's direction. "Did you just say you'd like Oliver to stay with us? I hope that's not what you said, sister. I hope I just misheard what you said just now."

"No, sister, you heard my words precisely," Charlotte said. "I do think Oliver *should* stay here…with us."

In that moment, it was hard to tell whose face held a greater expression of surprise.

Both Lillian and Ruth stared at Charlotte with their mouths hanging open.

"Are you sure, sister?" Ruth finally asked, stepping between Charlotte and Lillian. "Ever since we took Oliver in you've been complaining to me about how chaotic the house has been. You even said two cats in one house was simply not going to work. What has Oliver done to melt your heart?"

"You know, Ruth," Charlotte began, "the last day or two I was thinking about when we were girls. I was thinking back to how our mother demanded we act more like young ladies than children. Silence at the dinner table. Silence when we read at bed time. Silence in the morning before school. Because of our mother, I think silence just became something we grew accustomed to maintaining around here. It seems to me that a house is made for activity, noise and energy…not just silence. This morning, after reflecting on our last few days with Oliver here, that's what I was reminded of. Whenever I would watch Oliver and Mezzo romp around this house together, I was reminded of the joy that comes from living in an active house…not a quiet one."

"But two cats?" Ruth laughed.

"I know," Charlotte smiled, "but a little disorder around the house isn't the worst thing, sister. Life isn't about being quiet and organized all the time. Of course, this house will be a little less quiet but I'm okay with that…if you're okay with it, sister."

Ruth looked at Lillian and then at the cat peering at her from inside the small cage.

"I…I'd suppose you're right," Ruth mumbled, before turning to Charlotte. "It has been nice having our house be a little more…lively. Since Oliver came it makes me smile watching him and Mezzo sprint around the house. They are like…two little children. However, I must insist we maintain some silence to sleep at night, Charlotte. I simply can't get a good night's rest with a cat meowing at all hours."

"We'll figure out a way to keep them quiet at night," Charlotte nodded.

"All right then, Charlotte," Ruth sighed. "Let's add another member to our family."

Lillian quietly placed the carrying case down on the front lawn and opened the cage. Without hesitation, Oliver leaped from the cage and charged up the steps of the front porch and darted right through the front door. A few seconds later, Mezzo appeared in the doorway, snapped her tail once and then turned and charged down the hallway after Oliver. Charlotte turned to Ruth and smiled.

"Like you said, sister, an active home is a happy home."

Chapter 27:  ONE WEEK LATER

St. John's Episcopal Church has a few unique distinctions among all the churches in Washington D.C. First, it's location makes it the closest church to the White House. Second, it is also the only church that can lay claim to having had every president since James Madison attend at least one service during their term as President. These are two special details that Charlotte and Ruth are well aware of. Having attended St. Johns all of their lives, they have grown quite accustomed to seeing Presidents in person, especially when sitting in a pew at their church.

One Tuesday afternoon, right after lunch, Ruth and Charlotte decided to walk to St. Johns church. However, unlike when they go on a Sunday, their church was empty when they arrived. Silence filled the sanctuary when they stepped inside. Standing near the altar it appeared to be just the Dupree Sisters and God for a few quiet moments.

A few days earlier, Ruth asked Charlotte if they could stop in the church on another day during the week. When Charlotte agreed, she overheard Ruth call Reverend Simmons on the phone to ask if he could leave the church unlocked for them. This sparked a few questions in Charlotte's mind, but she thought it best to wait and see what her sister was up to.

From the moment they arrived at the church, and stepped into the vacant sanctuary, Charlotte was still uncertain about what Ruth's motivation was for this visit. She followed Ruth to their usual pew and they sat down together and stared at the altar.

"Are we here to meet with Reverend Simmons?" Charlotte asked.

"Not exactly," Ruth replied, adjusting the kneeler to their pew.

"Then why are we here?" Charlotte asked in a softer tone of voice.

"Because a young girl named Maria Nunez died," Ruth whispered.

With those words, Ruth quickly got down on both knees, folded her hands and looked up to heaven. Charlotte managed to also get down on both knees, but before folding her hands she turned to Ruth, who was simply staring at the stained-glass window behind the altar.

"Why are we here?" Charlotte asked.

"I keep thinking about her," Ruth admitted.

"Who?" Charlotte asked.

"Maria Nunez," Ruth replied.

"The maid?" Charlotte asked.

"I can't help it," Ruth stated. "I know she showed poor judgment in blackmailing a Representative, but when we were in our early twenties…I'm quite certain we made mistakes both big and small."

"So true," Charlotte nodded.

"You know I made some phone calls about Maria," Ruth continued.

"To whom?" Charlotte asked.

"I called the employment agency that recommended her," Ruth replied, her eyes still fixed on the altar. "The woman I spoke to said that Maria did not have any family or social security number in her file. So I guess she was here illegally."

"That's what Mr. White said," Charlotte nodded. "Another woman coming here trying to pursue the American dream I'm sure."

Ruth grew silent and stared at the front of the church where a stained-glass image of Jesus looked back at them.

"You know why I can't stop thinking about this, sister?" Ruth explained. "It seems to me that when Maria died somewhere in this world a mother lost her daughter...her child...and she'll never know about it. Somewhere in the world there's a mother who lives in another country who thinks Maria is still working hard and will become successful in America one day. She won't ever know what happened or that Maria is dead. I just thought...someone should pray for Maria Nunez. Her mother won't know to do it. That's why I wanted to come here, sister. I wanted to pray for the soul of someone's daughter because I don't think anyone else will."

After hearing those words, Charlotte folded her hands, closed her eyes and joined her sister in prayer. Together the Dupree Sisters remained in the pew with heads bowed. They prayed about the previous weeks and the lives that had been changed. They prayed for the one life that was lost. They prayed for forgiveness for all involved and they hoped that God was listening.

## Chapter 28: BACK TO BLAIR HOUSE

For the second time in less than a month, the Dupree sisters found themselves back at Blair House for another social event. It was a private party to recognize the service of a mutual friend who had volunteered her services to Blair House for thirty years. Marge Blouch had worked as a fundraiser to raise money for the preservation of Blair House. She had worked closely with many presidential administrations, but now she decided to move on to other interests in her life.

Stepping through the front door of Blair House, Ruth and Charlotte couldn't help but remember the last time they were there. It was a less than pleasurable experience being distracted by questions and thoughts about a murder. This time around, both Ruth and Charlotte were prepared for a more relaxed experience. After some smiles and kind words with fellow guests, Ruth headed right to the hors d'oeuvres and helped herself to a plate full of food. Charlotte, trailing behind Ruth, also picked up a plate for a few pieces of crab toast. As they walked away from the table, Ruth paused and looked at Charlotte.

"The salmon tastes flat," Ruth quietly observed after one bite of a small portion of salmon on a slice of cucumber. "When we were here a few weeks ago the salmon had a richer flavor to it."

Charlotte took a bite of her crab toast and slowly nodded her head.

"I notice the same thing with the crab," Charlotte said, gesturing to the items on her plate. "This crab toast just doesn't taste the way it did the last time we were here."

Both sisters turned to find the guest of honor, Marge Blouch, standing beside them. She stared at the sisters while squeezing her hands together in front of her waist. A smile appeared and she took a step towards them.

"Hello, Marge," Ruth smiled.

"Congratulations, Marge," Charlotte grinned. "You certainly gave Blair House a lot of time and energy over the years. They couldn't put a price on all the fundraising you helped with. They will miss you."

"I agree," Ruth nodded before taking another bite of salmon and cucumber.

"Thank you," Marge smiled. "I'm so glad you two could come. It's a special day so enjoy yourselves. I see you've already found something to eat."

"Yes," Charlotte began. "My sister and I were just commenting on how the food tastes…different. We had these same hors d'oeuvres a few weeks ago, yet they don't taste the way they did on our last visit."

"There's a reason for that," Marge nodded. "We lost our chef about a month ago and we've been struggling to find a replacement."

"Really?" Charlotte asked. "Did he find work elsewhere? I mean I'd think that preparing meals for former presidents and dignitaries would be a job worth keeping. Why would anyone stop working at Blair House?"

"He died," Marge replied.

"Oh," Charlotte sighed.

"Is that a good enough reason, sister?" Ruth grinned, elbowing Ruth in the side.

"What happened?" Charlotte asked.

"Security found him on the kitchen floor one evening," Marge recalled. "They say he died of a massive heart attack. When something like that happens, it makes you think. At least it made me think. That's when I decided to step away from Blair House."

No one spoke for a few seconds after hearing such an unusual explanation.

"Well…I'm sorry about your chef," Charlotte said, breaking the silence.

"Yes…that is a shame," Ruth chimed in.

"It is," Marge explained, glancing around the room at the other guests. "He was a large man with a pension for working more than he exercised. Being a chef and working around food all day, I'd suppose he simply indulged his pallet a bit too much. So far they've interviewed quite a few candidates to replace him. They're really taking their time hiring someone. So until we find a replacement, we bring in chefs from around town to fill in with varying results."

"How many interviews have been done?" Charlotte asked.

"Quite a few," she replied, turning her eyes to Charlotte.

"Do they cook meals as part of the interview?" Ruth asked.

"I think they do that after the first interview," Marge nodded. "At the moment, from what I understand, they've been talking to candidates. I also learned that they're putting a special emphasis on discussing the rules about cleanliness in the kitchen."

"What do you mean by…cleanliness?" Ruth asked.

"Didn't the last chef wash his hands enough?" Charlotte asked.

"It wasn't that," Marge explained, and she drew in her breath and glanced at both sisters. "You see, the last chef had this terrible habit of bringing his cat to work with him. He'd actually drop scraps of meat on the floor for his cat to eat. It was a filthy habit, in my opinion. Since he didn't have any family, I suppose that cat was like his child. I heard he'd even crack open a window in the kitchen to let the cat run in and out all day long. He treated that cat like his only child. Perhaps that's why he decided to name the cat after himself."

"And what was the chef's name?" Ruth asked.

"Oliver Tuck," Marge replied.

Charlotte dropped her appetizer on the floor when she heard the name. She quickly reached down and scooped it up with one hand.

"So the cat's name was?" Charlotte asked, dumping the crumbs on her plate.

"Oliver," Marge replied and she shook her head. "While the staff appreciated Chef Tuck's work, his habit of keeping a pet in the kitchen with him was something they didn't appreciate. I heard they found him right there on the kitchen floor. No sign of his cat, though. In fact, I don't think anyone knows what ever happened to that cat."

"Well, Marge," Charlotte smiled, "I guess it's just another Washington mystery."

"Hopefully a mystery with a happy ending," Marge replied.

Charlotte smiled and nodded to the comment and glanced over at Ruth.

"Yes," Charlotte grinned. "If there's one thing Ruth and I like it's a happy ending."

## THE END

## ABOUT THE AUTHOR

 Allen B. Boyer is the author of two Young Adult novels and one nonfiction book about the West Point Academy and its famous graduates. His books have been sold around the country. His Bess Bullock Retirement Home Mystery series produced five books for Cozy Cat Press. *Death at the Presidents Church* began his new Dupree Sisters Mystery series. This book is the second in that series.

Mr. Boyer lives near Hershey, Pennsylvania, with his wife, Suzanne, and their three children. He likes to take his children and their dog to visit residents at a nearby retirement home.

www.ingramcontent.com/pod-product-compliance
Lightning Source LLC
Chambersburg PA
CBHW020329260626
47156CB00004B/1437